the Gold Armband

Jeanne K. Norweb

Katewood Books

To
Shirley and all my Extended Family
"May we all meet one day beyond the Blue Road"

THE GOLD ARMBAND
Cover and illustrations by M. Caruso

Katewood Books
26 Harmony School Rd.
Flemington, NJ 08822

First Printing, 2007
Printed in the United States of America

SAPH

CONTENTS

the

Gold

Armband

CHAPTER 1
Alan's Picnic

After mailing a package for their mother, the Hartland twins, Gregory and Marilyn, walked over to the largest store in the seaside village to which they had moved from Liverpool the previous year. The owner, Mr. James, and his eldest son, Tom, a young man of twenty-four, were changing the display in the window. The twins waved to Tom, who waved back and went on working. In the store behind him they could see the rest of the James family, busy arranging the counters. Alan James, a boy Greg's and Lyn's age, was helping. It always amazed Lyn that Alan, who had been born blind, could do so many things and that he never complained or felt sorry for himself.

"I don't see how he does it," Lyn had once confided to her brother. "If I were like that I would be an abyss of self-pity."

"So would I," her sports-loving brother had agreed with a slight shiver.

As they watched the window display take shape, they discussed their plans for the next day.

"Let's go to Smugglers' Cove," Lyn suggested. "I suppose we'll be disappointed again for about the hundredth time, and the Door won't be there, but I love the place anyway."

"So do I. Even though nothing happens, it always has a mysterious, all-alone air."

"Hello," said a cheerful voice beside them. "What makes Smugglers' Cove mysterious?"

It was Alan.

"Tom told me you were watching. Come on in. We are almost through and about to have a snack."

"Why do you feel that Smugglers' Cove is mysterious?" Alan asked again when they were perched on empty crates and eating apples. "I've always felt that way about it. Just hearing the name 'Smugglers' Cove' makes me think of all the exciting adventures that must have taken place when it really was used by smugglers. I've always wanted to go there."

"You could come with us," Lyn said, then added hesitatingly, because their uncle doctor had told them that besides being blind, Alan had heart trouble, "we would love to have you come, but it's a pretty long walk from here and a bit of a scramble down to the beach."

Tom glanced at his brother's wistful expression. "Look here, I'll run you all over there in my boat tomorrow. We can take a spin up the coast and then I'll leave you in the Cove while I visit a friend and pick you up later."

"The friend's name is Ellen, isn't it?" said Mr. James with a jovial laugh in which all the family joined.

"I'll fix a picnic for you," said Mrs. James.

"Wonderful! Thank you so much!" exclaimed the twins. A ride in Tom's motorboat was always fun

4

and Mrs. James' picnic baskets were noted for being filled to overflowing.

On their way home Lyn paused in front of a handsome house. "I wish we could afford a place like this," she said to her brother.

He looked at her in surprise. "What has come over you? You were delighted when we bought the house we were renting. Count on a girl to change her mind," he said loftily and walked on. "Humph! I think that visit to your fancy friends has turned your head."

"Of course it hasn't," Lyn retorted. Yet it was true. Until her recent visit to a very wealthy classmate, she had loved their small, white house with its colorful windowboxes and trim garden which had been transformed from a weed patch into a floral bouquet by her mother's green thumb. But for ten days she had been surrounded by unaccustomed luxuries; servants to wait on her, horses to ride, beautiful gardens to wander through and nothing to do except amuse herself. Her friend's mother had even let her try on some extremely valuable jewelry. She had returned wishing they were, well, not necessarily as rich as her friend's family, but much richer than they were. Since then, she had wasted a good deal of time in daydreams in which she either earned a tremendous reward by some heroic deed or else discovered one of the hidden treasures which local tradition said had long ago been buried in the area by buccaneers.

She had never told these daydreams to Greg and therefore, to divert his attention, she proposed a race home. "Or rather, you can trot along beside me while I run."

Greg laughed and patted her teasingly on the head. "Certainly, my little sister."

"Younger by only twenty-five minutes," she retorted, laughing also. Though unlike in both looks and temperament, they got on well together, and this was one of their standing jokes.

When they met Tom and Alan at the wharf the next day, Lyn had a small bouquet of flowers she had picked in her mother's garden. "They are for Ellen," she told Tom, "as a 'thank you' for our outing."

Tom was extremely pleased and gave them a grand ride. They circled several small boats at anchor, then went out to sea and exchanged waves with a passing ship, and after that ran up the coast. Then Tom headed to Smugglers' Cove. He nosed the boat towards the shore until the prow gently touched bottom.

"Take off your shoes and socks," he said. "You can wade in."

Lyn had noticed that he always let Alan be as independent as he could.

"Drop off here, Alan," he said when Alan sat down on the prow. "Then go in the direction you are facing now."

Greg and Lyn followed, carrying the basket. They stood waving as the boat backed off and sped out of the cove.

"Your brother is wonderful!" Lyn exclaimed.

"He's my favorite brother. The others are won-

rful also, but Tom makes me feel that I can do just
out anything by myself."

"We will do the same," Greg promised. "Now,
at do you want to do first? Eat or wade or
at?"

Alan was not paying attention. "Hush," he said,
appeared to be listening intently to something.
ou are right. It *is* a mysterious place. So quiet and
so awake, as though it were guarding a secret."

Lyn and Greg were startled. The cove did indeed
rd a secret, but how did Alan know? True, the
sea was dead calm and there did seem to be a
special quietness about the cove, but that was all.
They looked at each other excitedly. Perhaps the
Door was waiting for them. Lyn darted to the cave
and looked in, then shook her head sadly at her
brother.

Greg said, "This place must have lots of secrets
to keep. Just think of how the smugglers must have
been in constant fear of the King's men finding them
here and capturing them. Most likely there were
some bloody skirmishes on these very sands."

"Perhaps it is guarding buried treasure," Lyn
said hopefully. "If only we could find it, how rich
we would be! Why, there might be chests of jewels
and gold!"

"This place has probably been dug up dozens of
times by people who had the same idea," said Greg.
He had a tendency to throw cold water on schemes.

"Maybe they stopped just short of finding it,"
insisted his sister.

Alan shook his head. "I didn't mean that type of

secret. I don't know how to explain it; but it *is* guarding a secret. I know it is; and I am right in the middle of it." He laughed. "Can't you feel it? It's all over the place."

He sat down and put on his shoes and socks. "I want to explore. Is the beach smooth or rocky?"

"Smooth," answered Greg. "In the back the cliffs come down straight to the sand except in one spot near the end where the cliffs have tumbled down long ago. Lyn and I have climbed up there but it is pretty steep. Then on either side there are rocks that reach out like arms into the sea."

"They are guarding that secret," said Alan. He got up and Greg took him over to the cliff, where with one hand touching it, he began to walk along it.

"I'll put the basket in the cave out of the sun," said Lyn. She carried it to the cave and put it just inside the opening, then gave an exclamation. The Door they had longed to see was now in the back of the cave.

Alan's quick ears heard the sound. "What is it?"

"Nothing," said Lyn, trying to keep the excitement out of her voice. She gesticulated wildly in order to catch Greg's attention, then putting her finger to her lips, beckoned to him. He guessed at once what had happened and dashed over. After a quick look over his shoulder to see that Alan was not near any rocks, he hurried with Lyn into the cave.

"What shall we do? We can't take Alan with us. He couldn't see anything anyway, and might get hurt," Lyn whispered into her brother's ear.

"Of course he can't come with us. Much too dangerous. Besides, we would have to stay with him all the time, and then how could we do anything? But, after all, we can leave him here. No matter how long we are beyond the Door, we will come back here at exactly the same moment we left. Alan won't have taken one step further."

Lyn nodded. They peered around the edge of the cave. Alan was still feeling his way along the base of the cliff, and there was nothing except smooth sand before and behind him.

"Quick," Greg murmured. He dashed over to the Door and pushed. Nothing happened. He pushed harder. Still nothing happened. Finally he threw his weight against it. The Door remained shut. Lyn added her weight though she knew it would do no good.

They stared perplexedly at the Door and then at each other. "If we aren't supposed to go through it, why is the Door here?" demanded Greg. "We were never told that we couldn't go back again. On the contrary, when the Master of Wisdom said good-bye to us, he sounded as though he expected us to return some day."

Lyn thought for a moment, then said slowly, "I wonder if our decision to leave Alan behind is the reason. Perhaps he is the one who is meant to open the Door this time."

"Do you mean that perhaps we won't be allowed to go through, only Alan?" Greg exclaimed in dismay. "How could he get along without us?"

"I hope we are supposed to go through also, but we have to take Alan with us."

"You might as well go ahead and say we were being selfish," Greg replied, a trifle sulkily because he suspected Lyn was right. "But I still think it's much too dangerous for him. He will undoubtedly be terrified of dragons, and what shall we do then?"

Lyn paid no attention to his sulkiness. She ran out of the cave and over to Alan who had nearly reached the end of the beach.

"Come!" she cried excitedly, catching hold of his hand. "We want to show you something in the cave."

She led him to the back of the cave. "What do you feel right there in front of you?" she demanded.

"It feels like a door. Is this where the smugglers kept their loot? Where's the handle?"

"It's a swinging door."

Alan gave the Door a slight push. It swung open at once, letting the bright light of the dragons' land pour into the cave.

"What has happened? Where does this door lead to? Where are we?" Alan cried out, starting forward with his hands in front of him.

Greg and Lyn were right behind him, afraid that the Door would swing shut and leave them behind. Not that we could go through it if we were not supposed to, Lyn thought.

Alan stopped in the grassy glade. "Where am I?" he said again in amazement. "It feels like sunlight, but not like ours. This pours right into me," he ended softly.

"We will tell you. Yes, it is sunlight and we're in a glade. Come here and sit down and we will explain what has happened."

They guided Alan into the shade of one of the huge trees on the edge of the glade and they all sat down on the grass.

"We're in another world," Lyn began, and then she and Greg in turn told Alan about their visit to the land of the Green Dragons.

Alan did not seem at all surprised. "Another world! Touching ours in some way . . . a world we are sometimes allowed to enter through the Door that is between them. I knew there were places like this, I knew it!" he cried out triumphantly. "The land of the Green Dragons! Tell me more about it!"

The twins did. They told him of how when they were there previously, the kingdom had fallen into disorder because of weak kings, and that King Damor had brought peace to the kingdom after a terrible war with the Dark Dragons who scoffed at the laws of the Great One.

"I wonder why the Door was put there for us this time?" Alan remarked. "There must be a special reason."

"There was the last time," said Greg. "We'll just have to wait and find out."

"I wonder how long it is since we were here? Laura and David Manley, Captain Manley's grand-children, were here before we came," Lyn added, laughing, "and it was so strange to hear the dragons tell about their having been here generations previously when we knew it was only the year before, in

11

our world."

"Come on!" said Alan, jumping up with a joyous shout. "I want to meet the dragons!"

Greg told him, "First we have to get out of this forest. Once we get to that large meadow with the big, winding river – that is where Lyn stepped on the dragon's tail – we may be able to see a flying dragon and signal to him."

He spoke confidently but Lyn was apprehensive. Suppose there was a bad king on the throne; or one who did not want strangers in his kingdom? Suppose he was angry at their coming? But she kept these thoughts to herself for fear of frightening Alan, and only mouthed silently to Greg that they should reconnoiter first before letting the dragons see them. He nodded back 'yes' as he took Alan's arm, saying, "You're going the wrong way, Lyn, the meadow is in this direction."

"No, that is too far to the right. I am sure it is over this way."

"You're wrong. I've done cross-country running and I know how to put a course in my head. You haven't."

"This time you're wrong," Lyn insisted stubbornly. They might have ended up in one of their occasional endless arguments if Alan had not stopped them by saying, "Why not aim at halfway between the two points you are claiming are the right ones? If the meadow is so large we'll probably hit it. Anyway, let's start going somewhere."

At first they went slowly as the ground in this part of the forest was uneven, and huge, twisted roots rose out of the ground in unexpected places. Besides, Alan kept begging them to stop and be quiet so he could just listen. "The birds are different here," he would say. "Do you hear that one? I've never heard one like it before," or he would surprise them with remarks such as, "I think it must be mid-summer here. Everything smells that way, not fresh like spring or early summer." Then he would turn his head and say, "What is that fragrance coming from over there?" and Lyn would bring him a flower or herb to touch and smell.

Most of all, though, he wanted to hear about the dragons, what they looked like, what they did, and about the purple dragon who was the Master of Wisdom, and who lived on the small mount from which one could see, day and night, the Blue Road which led Home to the Great One.

Talking excitedly, they went on until they came to an open, wet area dotted with bright green tufts of grass. None of them had ever seen a bog though they had heard of them, and so when Greg saw an unusual purple flower, he said, "Look at that flower! I'll get it for you, Alan," and started leaping from tuft to tuft. About ten feet from the edge, one gave way under him. He fell into the mud and to his horror found no solid ground.

Luckily he did not panic and managed to struggle to a nearby fallen log, got his arms around it, and then heaved himself astride it.

At first Lyn did not realize what had happened. "What are you doing?" she asked.

"It's a bog, and there's no bottom. Don't come

near it."

"How are you going to get back?"

"I don't know. See if you can find a long log."

"Rescuers use ladders to save people on thin ice or quicksand," said Alan. "Maybe we could find branches and crisscross them."

"Good idea, Alan. See what you can do, Lyn."

Lyn left Alan safely by a tree and hurriedly searched. Hot and perspiring, she was dragging back the largest fallen branches she could find when a voice behind her said, "Who are you and where do you come from? I have never seen anyone like you before."

Lyn dropped the branches and spun around. One of the long, lizard-like creatures the dragons call their Dragon-Cousins, though there is no relationship between them, was eyeing her.

"We came through the Door, the one that is forbidden to you but not to us. We were trying to find the big meadow, the one that has the wide, twisting river flowing through it, when my brother fell into the bog. Please help me get him out."

"Hmmm," said the Dragon-Cousin, casting a glance at Greg on his log. "He is safe enough for the moment. What were you going to do when you got to that meadow?"

"Once out in the open we hoped to see a dragon who would be good enough to carry us . . . to the King, of course," she added hastily, remembering the wartime conditions of their first visit and not wanting him to think they were spies. "Do please help us."

The Dragon-Cousin ambled over to the bog and unconcernedly began to walk across it with his broad body flat and his feet stretched out.

Astonished, Lyn watched him. "Why, he's the same effect as a ladder," she said to Alan as she explained what was happening.

In a few moments the Dragon-Cousin was alongside Greg.

"Get on my back," he said. Then, as Greg cautiously inched himself off the log and onto the broad back, "Do you have to take all day doing it?"

He crawled back to the solid land and interrupted the children's thanks with, "Now, try to be more intelligent the next time and remember what a bog looks like when you see one."

He said he would guide them to the meadow and stay with them until they met some dragons. In that way they would not get lost again.

Greg suspected he was doubtful of these strange newcomers' real intentions and wanted to make certain they were taken straight to the King, so he said, "My sister and I are the Greg and Lyn who were here at the beginning of King Damor's reign. You must have heard of us."

"Are you really that Lyn and Greg? King Damor lived seven reigns past, but of course, I have heard of you. Everyone has!" exclaimed the Dragon-Cousin. "If you are, the King will certainly welcome you."

This was reassuring. "What is the King like?" Lyn asked. "Poor Damor had to fight and struggle so hard to straighten out his father's and grandfather's negligence."

"We have an excellent King," said the Dragon-Cousin. "A little stern, perhaps, but he is just, conscientious, well-liked and trusted. His son will undoubtedly also be a good king after him."

Before they could ask more questions, the trees ended abruptly and they found themselves on the edge of the large meadow.

"Now I know where we are. I recognize that hill to the left. The palace must be over there," Greg said, pointing to the west. "Can you see any sign of a dragon, Lyn?"

CHAPTER 2
King Tolmar

They walked out into the meadow and were so eagerly searching the sky ahead that they did not see the two dragons who came gliding over the trees behind them, until they closed their wings and dropped down in front of them.

Their coming was so swift and sudden that Lyn gave a little scream of surprise.

"Halt!" thundered the first dragon. "Who are you and why do you come to the land of the Green Dragons?" He looked fierce and on his sides were scars from battles. Around his neck was a gold and ruby collar, and so the twins knew at once that this was the King. The second had only the gold armband which all the Green Dragons and Dragon-Cousins wear.

"Hail, Your Majesty," said Greg, stepping forward and bowing low. Lyn did the same. She nudged Alan and whispered, "Bow. Dragons understand bows."

"We've come through the Door from England," Greg began.

"England!" exclaimed the second dragon, whom Lyn saw was much younger than the King. He sounded disappointed. "I thought you might have come from a place called Earth."

17

Lyn and Greg both laughed, their fears gone. "England is a place on Earth," Greg explained. "We are Lyn and Greg, the Children from Earth, who were here when King Damor had to win back this kingdom from the Dark Dragons who had invaded it."

"We beg to be allowed to visit your kingdom again," said Lyn with another and lower bow. She had forgotten Alan, who was behind her.

Now he cried out excitedly, "Are you dragons?" He did not sound the least bit frightened. "And are you the King? You sound just the way I thought you would – so regal. Your Majesty," he said, stepping forward and bowing. "Please let us stay for a while. I've always thought there must be worlds beyond our own, but I never dreamed there was one like this. Besides," he went on, going closer to the King, "since the Door is only there sometimes on our side, there must be a reason for our coming, and surely we are meant to stay here until we find out why. Doesn't Your Majesty think so?" He finished with another bow and the twins stared at him in amazement. They vividly remembered how afraid at first they had been of the dragons.

"It's different. He can't see," Greg mouthed to his sister. But Lyn was not so sure that was the reason. Alan's mother always said that "he sees farther than most people," and she suspected that Alan had at once sensed the atmosphere of goodness and peace of this land.

The King bowed his head. "I welcome you in the name of the Great One and so does my Queen. So you are Greg, and you are Lyn," he said, looking at each one of them in turn. "What is the name of your friend who longs to remain here? I see there is no fear in him," he ended with a slight chuckle.

"His name is Alan," said Lyn, wondering if she should mention that he was blind.

"I cannot see you," said Alan, going still closer to the King, "but please, might I touch you? That will give me an idea of what you look like. I wish I could see you." He gave a sigh. It was the nearest thing to a complaint that Lyn had ever heard him make. "But perhaps not being able to see you is, in a way, more exciting. If I saw you, I might see only the outside, and not the real you. If you understand what I mean."

The King nodded gravely, then bent down his head close to Alan's. "Yes, seeing with eyes is good, but seeing with the heart is better." He touched Alan gently, and Alan just as gently ran his hands along the King's face.

"Now," said the King, "we shall go back to the palace. I will carry two of you and my nephew, Lorimon, will take the third."

The children thanked the Dragon-Cousin for his help. Then Greg helped Alan climb onto the King's back, mounted behind him and said reassuringly, "I can steady you if necessary, but don't worry. It's easy to hang on and flying is great fun."

Alan grinned as he settled himself on the King's back. "I can't wait to find out what flying is really like! I mean flying with the wind blowing all around you and the sun shining on you, and then perhaps getting wet, passing through a cloud! One misses so much shut up in a plane!"

Lyn ran over to Lorimon and happily scrambled onto his back. They need not have worried about Alan. He would fit right in. He would love the dragons and they would love him and make certain that he came to no harm. She felt like singing and cheering as they took off and she saw the familiar landscape unfolding beneath her as they gained height. Only now did she realize how much she had missed it. She took a deep breath; they were going to have a wonderful time.

"You sound glad to be back," Lorimon said, turning his head around to look at her.

"I am. You simply cannot imagine how many times Greg and I have gone back to the cave hoping the Door would be there, but it never was until today. We were afraid that we were never going to be allowed to return."

"Were you really here when the Dark Dragons invaded our kingdom and captured the Princess Edrina?"

"Yes, we were, and we'll tell you all about it. It *is* exciting to look back on, but it was more frightening than exciting when it was actually happening. Have the Dark Dragons ever attempted another invasion?"

"There have been times when a bold or crafty Dark King has indeed tried to conquer us, but has never succeeded. We dragons have never forgotten the price we had to pay in the time of King Damor for our long carelessness. The border has been quite peaceful for several passings except for an occasional raid or skirmish. There was a particularly severe attack last summer but . . . well, they were driven off." He ended abruptly as though he had suddenly remembered something disagreeable; or else, thought Lyn, as she leaned forward to catch a glimpse of his face, something that worried him.

"Are you one of the Border Guard?"

"Yes, I am stationed at the southernmost post."

"Is that where the attack took place?"

"No. It was in the north. I was not there, my brother was. Here we are at the palace."

This time there could be no mistaking the abruptness with which he changed the subject. Lyn, however, did not have time to wonder about it as they had landed and the King was welcoming them again. He introduced them to the Queen who was a pleasant, kindly dragoness. Next they met the Crown Prince, also pleasant, but stodgy, the twins agreed when sharing their impressions later with each other. His wife, the Crown Princess, was, on the contrary, lively and charming. Their small son was healthy and active, though as yet unable to speak plainly. He showed such an interest in the newcomers and crawled around them so rapidly that his nurse finally removed him after Alan had nearly tripped over him, though Alan begged her not to.

The Queen asked if they would like refreshments, saying, "I seem to remember from the tales about you that you eat more frequently than we do, like our Dragon-Cousins."

"They never forget our eating habits," Greg murmured to Alan while Lyn politely accepted for them all.

By the time the refreshments had arrived, carried on the back of a Dragon-Cousin, several other dragons and Dragon-Cousins had joined the group. They had heard of the arrival of the famous visitors and so the rest of the day was spent in conversation. The twins wanted to be caught up on what had happened since they left, and the dragons wanted to hear about King Damor and his battle to restore the kingdom. When Lorimon understood that they had returned to their world before Damor could fulfill his promise of taking them all over the kingdom, he begged to be allowed to do it. The King gave permission at once. "It is a privilege to be able to grant the desire of one of my famous ancestors," Lorimon told them with obvious satisfaction.

After they had had their breakfast the next morning, they started off. As they gained height, Lyn caught sight of the Blue Road stretching from the land to the horizon, rippling and brilliant in the early morning sun.

"The Blue Road first, Lorimon," she begged. "Oh! How I have missed it!"

"You cannot imagine how many times we have both stood looking at the sea and wishing we could have even just a glimpse of it," added Greg.

When they landed, Greg helped Alan climb down and was going to lead him to the shore, but Alan, unaided, went unhesitatingly to where the Blue Road washed against the shore in ripples of blue light.

"I can feel it – but what is it like?" he asked.

"It is blue, blue," Greg began, then remembered that Alan did not know what blue was.

"And the light seems to be coming from within the ripples," said Lyn. But Alan lived in a world of darkness.

Alan leaned down and let the water flow over his hand. "It is so alive! Not slow-moving like our own sea," he said, wonderingly. "It is as though it were trying to tell me something."

"The Master of Wisdom will know how to explain it to him," said Lorimon. "We will go to the Mount."

The Master welcomed them kindly. Lyn, however, could not help feeling sad when she remembered the Master she had known and loved.

"You are sorrowful, Child from Earth," the Master said gently to her.

"I can't help missing the Master we knew."

"He was one of our great Masters," said the purple dragon, "and his love for you and your brother is told of in our tales. Love never dies but meets again beyond the Blue Road. Let that comfort your heart, Child from Earth."

"Master, could you help Alan in some way to 'see' the Blue Road, in his mind?" Lyn asked. "It is so beautiful. I had hoped that somehow its light would get through his blindness. But it didn't."

"There are many kinds of darkness, and the worst is not that of the eyes. Come with me," he said to Alan. "Let us gaze on the Blue Road together."

He took Alan to the edge of the plateau and they looked out towards the sea for a long time. Sometimes they spoke, but mostly they stood silently. When Alan rejoined them, his face was alight. All he said, however, was, "You two go on with Lorimon. I'm staying here with the Master. He said I could."

So Lyn and Greg had a marvelous time flying all over the kingdom and the principality of the Dragon-Cousins. As the Dragon-Cousin they had met in the forest said, the kingdom was at peace and the King was a careful and just ruler, and neither Greg nor Lyn could see any problems in which they might be involved.

"Well, I can't say that I'm sorry," Greg said one evening to Lyn. "We can just enjoy ourselves this time."

Every now and then they stopped at the Mount to see Alan, and after their first visit laughed at themselves for having been so reluctant to bring him. They had found him surrounded by young dragons and Dragon-Cousins who were listening wide-eyed to his tales. Lyn knew that Alan read Braille and listened to books on records, but she had no idea of what a gift he had for storytelling.

When he ended they called, "Hello!" to him across the little dragons' heads and he called happily back, "I hope you are having as good a time as I am!"

"We just stopped by to see if you wanted to come with us," said Lyn.

"No, thank you. I'm waiting to be taken to an

arm-banding ceremony. I'm going to tell stories afterwards. And then tomorrow I must go to a wedding."

"He is in great demand," said a dragoness who was nearby. "But it is not only for his tales; everyone loves him."

Lyn and Greg saw him off and then went on with their excursions. Lorimon was a delightful companion. He showed them everything he thought could possibly interest them, and they became very fond of him.

"When are we going to meet your brother?" Lyn asked him one day.

"He is stationed in the northernmost post near the sea. I will take you there tomorrow."

Dathir was a handsome young dragon with many gold markings, but he seemed restless.

"Nothing ever happens here," he said discontentedly in answer to Greg's questions as to whether there had been any recent attacks. "I think I am being kept here just because I asked to be transferred."

Lyn and Greg exchanged surprised glances. It was so unusual to hear a Green Dragon speak like that.

Lorimon said reprovingly, "Now, Dathir, be reasonable. You know you are being kept here because you are not yet fifty-five, and for no other reason." He noticed the children's puzzled expressions and explained, "Those who wish to be warriors may join the Border Guard when they come of age at fifty, but until they are fifty-five they are kept for training either with the Palace Guard or at one of the posts where there is almost never any action."

"But I have proved myself!" Dathir protested. "An exception should be made for me! You know everyone says that I can fight as well as a fully-trained warrior. Anyway, I am tired of doing nothing. My leave is coming up and so is yours, Lorimon. You know how we have always wanted to go north and see if we could discover where our ancestors came from and if there are still any dragonsthere. Now I mean to do it. Come with me."

Lorimon chuckled. "It is true," he said to Lyn and Greg. "When we were children we loved to hear the tale of how, uncounted generations back, a small group of dragons led by their King came from the north, or rather, I should say, fled from the north and settled here. Once when we were still quite small – I had not yet received my gold armband, and Dathir is seven passings my junior – we took some provisions and left without telling our parents. We got as far as the northern border and there, of course, were stopped by the Border Guard. By then we were so tired that we were relieved to be caught and taken back to our parents, even though we both received a good scolding."

"We haven't heard that tale! Do tell us!" Lyn begged.

"As I said, uncounted generations ago, the Green Dragons lived much farther north. They obeyed the laws of the Great One as we do now, but they did not wear the gold armband. How we came to wear it is another tale that has nothing to do with this one.

"The valley where they dwelt was pleasant and well-sheltered by mountains. They had no enemies and lived in peace. Perhaps too much so, for they never kept watch. So it happened one night when all slept, that a nearby mountain which they called 'Smoketop' because it was always smoking, broke into pieces and threw boiling rocks high into the air. A river of fire poured down its slopes and engulfed the nearest houses before the dragons, who had been awakened by the roar of the splitting mountain, could leap into the air. Parents snatched up their children and all fled as best they could, but in every direction there were screams of terror and agony as the hurtling rocks hit old and young and drove them down into the river of fire. Fortunately, King Tolmar lived across the valley. He was one of our great kings and even as he leapt into the air he looked for the best way to escape the peril. He realized that the wind bore fumes as death-dealing as the falling rocks and the fire below. So he flew out of the wind, calling loudly for all to follow him. Some did, but others in terror scattered far and wide.

"It was a sorrowful little company that the King led to safety. All had lost relatives or friends, and most were themselves sick from the fumes. When the mountain was at length quiet, the King sent back scouts who returned in great grief. Where the dragons had lived so happily, there was now a valley of hot, black stone. Every home had been engulfed by that river of flame. Several times scouts sought for survivors, but only twice brought back a few dragons whom they had found, who had also been searching for lost ones.

"King Tolmar then spoke to all the dragons: 'It is not possible for us to remain longer here. This place is not fertile, the hunting is poor, and there is little shelter to protect us, and especially our children, from the nearing winter. In the south as we all know is the great high pass through the mountains. It seems to beckon to me, and my heart tells me that we who obey the Great One will not be forsaken. In the South we shall find a land where we are to dwell.'

" 'How shall we know that we have found that place?' asked one of the dragons.

" 'There will be a sign.'

" 'What will be the sign?'

" 'I do not know, but we shall all know it when it comes.'

"The dragons were very loath to leave the land where they had dwelt in happiness for so long. But they recognized the wisdom of their King's words and knew that he spoke from the inner power which always comes with the kingship, and which good Kings use wisely, but poor Kings neglect. So they flew southward. It was a weary journey, for we dragons are not travelers by nature, and their pace was slowed by having to care for the very young and the few elderly who had managed to escape.

"When they found a pleasant valley they remained for a short while to rest. The tired group, who longed to have permanent homes once again, spoke of settling in that place, but the King spoke against it.

" 'No,' he said, 'this is not the place where our kingdom is to be.' Such was the power of his spirit, for as I said, he was one of our great kings, and so great was their trust in him, that all followed him ever southward.

"At last, one evening, they crossed these mountains in front of us and as soon as they dropped down, King Tolmar said, 'Here is where we are to stay.' The next morning when they flew up at sunrise to search for food, they saw the Blue Road. Whether it was there when they arrived the evening before or whether it appeared during the night was never known. Some said they thought they had caught a glimmer of it in the gathering darkness, but others were certain the sea had been empty. No matter. All knew this was the sign they had been waiting for, and so they remained here and the kingdom was established.

"Soon after their arrival the first Master of Wisdom came, but from where, he never said. King Tolmar welcomed him and gave the Mount to him and his successors to dwell on. He explained to the Green Dragons the purpose of the Blue Road and taught them many other wise and good things. That is why they called him the Master of Wisdom. He promised that as long as the dragons were faithful to the laws of the Great One, there would always be a Master to teach and comfort them. Together, this first Master and King Tolmar made the laws by which we have since lived, and also made the alliance with the Dragon-Cousins who were, as they are now, in the land south of us. From this time also they and we have worn the gold armband as a pledge to be faithful to the laws of the Great One, but that, as I said, is another tale."

"Hasn't anyone ever wanted to go back and see the place where you came from? Perhaps some of the Green Dragons did survive?" asked Greg. "In our world there would have been dozens of search parties and exploring expeditions by now."

Lorimon laughed. "As I told you, we Green Dragons are not travelers or explorers. We prefer to remain in our own realm, living quietly with our families. Every now and then, a more venturesome dragon has flown far north, but has always returned after having found nothing except higher and higher mountains and no sign of dragons, or even of the smoking mountain."

"Perhaps the mountain was not smoking when they were there. That type of mountain – we call them volcanoes – sometimes die out after a large eruption like the one you described. At other times they remain dormant for a while and then start smoking again. Even if it is extinct, there should be a huge crater that could easily be seen from the air. There are many in our world," Greg told the dragons, who were listening attentively.

"Would you recognize a . . . crater, did you call it?" Dathir asked eagerly.

"Of course," replied Greg confidently. Not that he had ever actually seen a crater except in pictures, but he was certain that he could identify one.

"They are like huge hollowed-out bowls in the

earth," Lyn added.

"Would you like to come with us?" Lorimon asked. He now sounded as eager as his brother. "Like Dathir, I too would like to attempt what we so often planned in our childhood, and with you who know what a crater looks like, we will have far better hope of succeeding than those who tried before us."

Lorimon's confidence in their ability to recognize a crater was very pleasant, so Greg accepted the invitation promptly. "Of course we will go with you. It will be great fun! Don't you think so, Lyn?"

Lyn agreed. Since other dragons had returned safely, she did not see anything particularly dangerous in flying north. Besides, it was the hottest summer any dragon could remember and the cooler weather of the mountains would be a relief.

"That is settled, then," said Dathir. "Meet me here the day after tomorrow, Lorimon, and bring whatever you think is necessary. We can start the next morning."

"Wait," said Lorimon. "We must first ask our uncle's permission."

"Why?" retorted Dathir, with a few puffs of smoke. "We can do anything we like during our leaves. There is no order not to fly north over the border. All of us along this border often fly deep into the mountains to hunt."

"It is not the same, and you know it," said Lorimon. "What you mean is that you do not want to risk his refusing permission."

Dathir twitched his tail angrily. "Ask him if you

feel it is necessary and, unless you have lost courage, follow me. I am going, whether you come or not. Unless," he added nastily, "you urge our uncle to forbid this adventure. It is a great nuisance at times," he said, ignoring his brother and speaking directly to the children, "when the King is also one's uncle – and an overcautious uncle at that."

"Stop that kind of talk at once!" cried Lorimon, angry in his turn. But Dathir had leapt into the air and was off with a noisy sweep of his wings.

Lorimon looked after him and sighed, his anger gone. "I fear for him," he said sadly.

"What is wrong with him?" asked Lyn.

"He has the makings of a great warrior, a far greater one than I shall ever be, and he knows this only too well. For one of his temperament, he has had too many compliments during his training period, and too much admiration from the younger dragons, especially the dragonesses, without any failures that would temper his successes. Yet all this might not have harmed him too much except for what happened during that severe attack last summer that I told you about.

"He was visiting a friend at the Border Station where it took place. He joined in repelling the attack and the seasoned warriors said he acquitted himself extraordinarily well for one still in training. Not only did he receive far more praise than was good for him, but also, unfortunately, some of his friends put it into his head that since he was so able and had so distinguished himself, he should be allowed to join the fighting warriors on the west border without waiting until he was fifty-five. He became convinced this was his due, and confidently asked our uncle to make this exception. I was present when he made this request, and though he expressed himself humbly enough, it was evident that he expected instant permission. He was stunned when our uncle, kindly but firmly, explained that not only would he not grant such a permission to any dragon, but especially could he not do so for his own nephew, as that might be considered favoritism.

"Dathir took the refusal badly. His pride was hurt at having to return unsuccessful to his friends. They are not malicious, merely young and as imprudent as himself, but certainly their ill-considered sympathy increased his resentment.

"Do not think," he ended earnestly, "that Dathir would disobey the King or the laws of the Great One. No, indeed, he wears his armband with great pride and listens with respect to the Master. But he has closed one corner of his mind to all reason."

"If the King refuses to let you go exploring, what will Dathir do?" Lyn asked anxiously. She could not imagine one of the warriors disobeying, and she was relieved when Lorimon answered promptly.

"He would not go, of course; but enough of this for the moment. There is much to do if we are to leave in two days. First, to my uncle."

The King gave permission. "So, after all your childhood discussions and plans you are finally going North! But why is Dathir not with you to ask in person?"

33

Lorimon did not answer.

The King shook his head. "He is determined to go and fears a refusal, I suspect."

"Yes, my uncle. Yet, if you had refused, he would not have gone."

"But he would have grown still angrier. Well, I have given my permission."

"I am hoping this journey will help him. I have always found that the air and loneliness of the high mountains clear one's mind, and make many things seem less important."

The King nodded gravely. "That may be. Let us hope so."

"Do you think Dathir could really be a great warrior some day?" Greg asked the King.

"He has exceptional skill for a young warrior, but that is not enough to make a great warrior. Agreat warrior is also wise and prudent and, perhaps most important of all, has learned to live in peace with both success and failure, and with failure more than success. I fear for Dathir when he has to face failure, as we all must do sooner or later."

CHAPTER 3
Flight to the North

The preparations for their journey were simple: one gourd which could be used as a cooking pot, and four more, two large and two small, for eating bowls, which were packed in a carrying basket along with a few remedies for emergencies. Lyn added a couple of shells they had been given to use as spoons, and Greg tucked in the fishing lines he had brought along in the hope that Tom would give them a chance to use them.

"You will need a carrying pad such as we use when flying long distances on the dragons," said a Dragon-Cousin who was helping them get ready. The children had seen them many times. This pad was fastened before and behind the dragon's wings with two pockets in front and two behind into which a Dragon-Cousin would slip his feet and so ride securely without scratching his dragon friend. A pad was found that had the right size pockets for Lyn's and Greg's legs. When Lyn begged for something to hang on to, the Dragon-Cousin dexterously fastened stout, cord-like handles to the pad for each of them.

"I never imagined riding on a dragon could be so comfortable," said Lyn, after she had tried it.

"Won't it be a nuisance for you to carry both of

us and the basket?" Greg said to Lorimon.

"Not at all. Besides, Dathir and I will share the weight. One will take the basket and the other will carry you two."

"It's going to be terribly cold in the mountains," said Greg. "The Queen has given me two lovely, soft skins, but there is no way of keeping them on while flying. You're clever with your hands, Lyn. Couldn't you make us some sort of capes?"

"I was wondering if I could. Do you have your knife?"

That was a needless question. Greg's knife, with its twelve attachments, was one of his most prized possessions, and ever since receiving it at Christmas, he had kept it in his pocket fastened by a chain to his belt.

Lyn drew the pattern for a simple, semi-circular cape on the skins with a charred stick and Greg cut them, or rather hacked them, out. With considerable ingenuity, Lyn managed to gather the neck edge, and the end result were two garments that some-what resembled the long capes which men wore on horseback in the days when there were no cars. She was especially proud of the buttons. They were huge peach pits through which Greg had drilled holes.

"Good for you, Lyn!" said her brother encouragingly. "How about hoods and mittens?"

"Easier than capes! And I will make them with the fur inside. They will be warmer that way." Then for good measure, she added two pouches with drawstrings. Greg fastened his to his belt and she tied hers to the carrying pad.

Before leaving, they flew to the Mount to tell Alan where they were going. Lyn knew he would not want to come with them, but she felt uncomfortable at his not being able to take part in what she felt was going to be a glorious excursion.

The Prince went with them to the Mount.

"I wish I were going with you," he said wistfully. "I asked my father, but he would not let me. My wife was very relieved." He chuckled. "But still, I would have liked to go with you."

When the Prince was out of hearing, Lyn expressed to the Master her astonishment at the Prince's display of adventuresome spirit. "He seems so . . . what we call stodgy . . . that I have often thought it was too bad that Lorimon was not to be the next king."

"It is foolish to think this one should be in that one's place," was the Master's answer, and Lyn understood that he was gently chiding her. "Do you know, that in this world, and your world, and every other world, each one is born at the right moment and in the right place and with a task to do? They may do it well, or poorly, or not at all; that choice is their's.

"This Prince will not be a great king, but a good one. He thinks much on these things and he knows his limitations. He will choose wise Councillors and the kingdom will prosper under his rule."

"By wise Councillors I suppose you mean those who understand best the laws of the Great One," Lyn said softly.

"Of course. All wisdom is contained in the laws of the Great One. Do not your leaders and those who counsel them know this?"

"Some do, I guess, and some don't, but I am afraid more and more don't."

"Then in the end they will fail and fall." This was said with such finality that Lyn knew there was nothing more to say.

The twins were alarmed when on inquiring for Alan, they were told he was ill. They ran over to the house of the dragoness with whom he stayed and found him in bed, with the dragoness fussing over him as though he were one of her own children. He looked so white and tired that Lyn was frightened and hurried over to him.

"What is wrong?" she asked, taking hold of his hand. "Do you feel very ill?"

"Don't worry about me," Alan said cheerfully. "I had one of my attacks. I've had them before. Your uncle always tells me to rest several days after having one. That is what I am doing now."

Lyn told him briefly about the coming expedition. She hated the thought of giving it up, but she felt responsible for him. After all, she and Greg had invited him to go to Smugglers' Cove.

"Would you like me to stay with you?" she said as cheerfully as she could.

"If you are worried about my being well taken care of, don't bother," said Alan with a grin. "Watch!"

He sat up in bed. At once the dragoness' head came over his shoulder and she gently pushed him down again.

"Now, my dear, lie quietly since that is what your own Healer told you to do."

She slid her body between him and the twins and gently ushered them out. "He must sleep for a while and then have a good, nourishing soup."

She sounded so like their mother that Lyn had to laugh and was greatly relieved. Nevertheless, she ran back to where the Master was lying, quietly gazing, as he did for hours at a time, over the land to the sea and the Blue Road.

"I am worried about Alan and wonder if I should stay behind with him."

"Do you want to go with the others?" he asked kindly.

"Terribly," she answered truthfully. "On the other hand, Greg and I are responsible for his being here."

The great purple dragon looked at her with an even kinder expression. "Go with peace of heart, Child from Earth. Your friend is recovering. It is not yet his time to take the Blue Road."

Though a weight was lifted from Lyn's mind, she looked at the Master with a troubled expression. "I had hoped being near the Blue Road would help Alan. That its water might give him his sight, and instead he has fallen ill while here."

"The Blue Road can give healing of mind and heart, but not of body, except at the end. Do you understand, Child from Earth?"

"I think so," she replied, and after saying farewell, walked slowly back to where the others were waiting for her.

They stopped at the palace just long enough to pick up the basket and found that most of the dragons and Dragon-Cousins who lived in or near the palace had gathered to see them off. Instead of onebasket there were now two. The second was packed to the brim with provisions.

"So you will not have to waste time hunting, at least for a day or two," said the palace cook.

It was large and looked. heavy. "Do you think you will be able to carry it?" Greg whispered to Lorimon.

He laughed and thanked the cook warmly; then he put his head through the loops of the two baskets and with a last farewell, they were off.

At the border, they found Dathir ready and anxious to start.

"My leave begins when I go off duty this afternoon. We can leave early in the morning."

Greg and Lyn spent the night at the house of one of the warriors. His wife disapproved of the expedition.

"It is a mad thing to do, my dears," she said as she prepared a nice dinner for them. "Going off with those two wild young dragons. Are you sure your mother would approve? I certainly would never let any of my children do such a thing."

Nevertheless she got up early and gave them a hearty breakfast.

"Do eat well, my dears. This may be your last good meal until you return, if you *do* return! Though my husband *does* say that Dathir is an excellent hunter – if there is anything to hunt way up on the top of those mountains where I am told everything is frozen!"

Though the children were well accustomed to flying on dragons, they had never done so in the mountains, and it took them an hour or two to get adjust to the manner in which the dragons used the air currents. Time and again they would set their wings like huge gliders and were borne up and down over gorges and slopes. Sometimes they glided up over a crest and then down the other side like a hair-raising roller coaster. If it had not been for the leg pockets and rope handles, Lyn and Greg would not have been able to stay on. Once or twice the dive was too steep and Lyn, who was in front, felt herself sliding forward and Greg coming on top of her; but at a warning shout, Lorimon would quickly straighten out and curve his neck back to see if they needed help.

At midday the dragons came down for a brief rest and to change the carrying pad from one to the other. The children barely had time to stretch their stiff legs and have a quick bite to eat before they were off again. By late afternoon they were tired and very cramped, and they asked Dathir to please drop down for a bit so they could stretch themselves.

"Just a bit further ahead," he said encouragingly. "We must go as far as we can each day."

'Just a bit further ahead' the children found out, meant the end of the day! When he finally landed, they tumbled off groggily and sat where they fell, clenching and unclenching their hands to get them limber, and bending and stretching their legs.

"You will feel less stiff tomorrow," Dathir said kindly.

Neither Greg nor Lyn wanted to disappoint their dragon friends by asking for more frequent rests. "We've never made a long flight before. We'll get used to it," Lyn said bravely, wondering if they ever would.

To their great relief, the next day was easier, even though they were flying farther and higher into the mountains.

"How do you know which way to go?" Greg asked when he noticed that the dragons never hesitated when they came to intersecting valleys or were faced with choosing between different passes through the mountains.

"From what we know of King Tolmar's journey, we think he probably always chose whichever valley or pass led more directly to the south, and so we are heading north in the same manner."

This route led them farther and farther inland, and at first was entirely in the mountains. The breeze made by the dragons' wingbeats, which had been pleasant and refreshing in the hot summer sky, now chilled them, especially their faces, though they pulled the edges of their fur hoods out like parkas. If they had not been warmed by the heat that came from the dragons' fire-filled bodies, they could not have stood it. When their faces became unbearably cold, they would lie along the dragon's back with their faces pressed first on one side of the dragon and then on the other.

Despite the dragoness' dire predictions, there was no lack of game, mostly wild goats and sheep, and fallen branches for firewood. The easiest and quickest way to prepare it, as Lorimon pointed out, was to make it into stew. The result was, as Greg ruefully put it, "Stew for breakfast, stew for dinner, stew for supper, and if we ever stopped in the afternoon it would be stew for tea, too!"

To the children's great relief, early on the fourth morning the mountains ended in an immense, warm plain that took the dragons a full day to cover. When they camped that evening, it was at the base of another and higher range of mountains. They slept, as they always did, with the dragons forming a protective circle around them.

Lyn awoke suddenly with the end of a long howl ringing in her ears. She jumped up as it came again, rising and falling, followed by a second and third howl. They were closer this time. The dragons were alert and watching. They had drawn the circle of their bodies tighter around the children.

"Wolves," said Greg, who had come over beside Lyn. They peered over Lorimon's back. A few minutes later came another howl, but much closer. Though the dragons made no movement to rise, Lyn could feel Lorimon's muscles tensing under his skin. A few more moments of waiting and the pack appeared. Lorimon waited until the head wolf was nearly upon him and then with perfect aim blasted him with a spout of flame. Dathir did the same to another wolf.

If the hunting howls had been frightening, it was nothing compared to the bedlam of howls and cries that now broke out. In a flash the pack was gone.

"Go back to sleep," said Lorimon. "They will not return. Dathir, it is your turn to watch." And he went to sleep.

By the next mid-day stop they were well into the new mountain range. The mountains were far higher and steeper than those of the first range, and the valleys were narrower and deeper. In one way this made the mountains more menacing, while on the other hand the depth of the valleys made flying easier, for the dragons, like humans, are affected by high altitude, though by no means as much. They breathed heavily as they went over the increasingly higher passes and came down to the valley floor on the other side panting, but they went on steadily. Their only fear was that they might have to turn back before discovering anything.

"We do not have to turn back when halfway through our leave," said Dathir. "Now that we know the way we will be able to return at a quicker pace."

Lorimon at first hesitated.

"After all," Dathir continued with a chuckle, "I have no more desire to be penalized for overstaying my leave than you do." Lorimon laughed and agreed.

"Lorimon, you were right. This journey has made a change in Dathir," Greg said when Dathir was out of earshot. "He has become such fun and never shows resentment anymore."

"Yes," replied Lorimon with a deep sigh of relief. "This is the way he used to be; generous and cheerful and never shirking his share of any work."

That might be true of Dathir, but it was a better description of Lorimon himself, Lyn thought privately. Lorimon was also endlessly kind to them and watched over them carefully. Not that Dathir was ever unkind, and he would have defended them to the death, but he rarely thought of their comfort, and he occasionally had a cocksure manner which annoyed her. When she expressed her preference for Lorimon to Greg, he defended Dathir whom he admired. "He has a certain 'dash' to him. There is nothing wrong with that, is there? But, you are right," he conceded, "Lorimon *is* more dependable."

One afternoon they came over the highest pass they had yet encountered and found themselves in a long, narrow valley that sloped steadily upwards. As it rose the side of the mountains grew steeper but there was no sign of a pass, only tremendously high, snow-capped peaks on either side and in front of them.

"We seem to be coming to a dead end," said Greg as twilight fell and the slopes began to grow white in the moonlight.

Lyn yawned. "Well, whatever we are coming to, I hope we stop soon. I'm getting sleepy and I'm afraid I shall fall off."

"We will drop down as soon as the moon touches those peaks," said Lorimon, nodding towards the western ridge.

The moon was hovering over the peaks when Dathir, who was flying ahead, called back, "Look! The valley does not end, but curves sharply!"

The dragons increased their speed and swept around the bend. A short way ahead the valley ended abruptly and, silhouetted in the moonlight, was a pass high between two, towering, snow-covered peaks.

"There is the high pass!" Dathir cried out, sweeping upwards. "We have found it at last!"

"It must be," Lorimon called up to him. "But come down. It would be too cold to attempt it tonight."

It was the coldest night they had yet spent. The dragons, used to a warm climate, did not like it at all; neither did the twins who were very thankful to have the warm sides of the dragons to curl up against. The dragons formed a tighter circle around them than usual, which somewhat protected them from the cold night breeze. But no one slept much.

In the morning, as soon as the sun had warmed the air a little, the dragons flew towards the pass which was so clear that it seemed deceptively near. They were soon panting from the exertion of flying sharply upwards in the unaccustomed thin air. The children likewise, even though they were sitting still, found breathing difficult.

Directly below the pass a steep cliff rose hundreds of feet from the valley floor to a broad, flat area like a small plateau. Another five hundred feet or so above it was the pass. The dragons landed on this flat space to discuss the difficulties of flying through the pass, because the dragons' wings, which are not as warm as their bodies, sometimes freeze when too long in icy conditions. After a few moments' conversation, Lorimon flew up to the pass, then came back breathing hard.

"The pass is not long," he reported. "There is, however, a strong, cold wind blowing through it. If we wait on this plateau until the sun is higher and has shone on it awhile, it will be warmer and very likely the wind will die down towards the middle of the day."

They waited. It was bitterly cold and the children alternated between doing mild exercises which left them gasping, and warming their hands and feet and faces on the dragons. Every now and then one or other of the dragons would leap into the air and fly around, beating his wings vigorously, and then come back.

"I think the sun is deliberately crawling up the sky today," said Lyn, stamping her feet and trying to laugh, though unsuccessfully, because her face was stiff from the cold.

At last Lorimon said, "Now get as warm as you can. We are going to attempt the pass."

They ran around and jumped up and down, then warmed their hands and faces and themselves against the dragons and climbed on. Since Dathir was carrying them, Lorimon took the lead. Lyn was glad that he would be the first one to see whatever lay beyond; she felt he deserved it.

She had never dreamed anything could be so cold as the pass. Though the wind had died down, there was still enough of it to chill her through. She felt she was turning into an icicle. The dragons breathed out fire on each side to warm their wings, and though the smoke made her cough, she was grateful for the blast of warm air. Fortunately the pass was not long, even to human eyes, and in a few minutes they were through and gliding down over sprawling foothills into a much lower – and warmer – valley than the one they had just left.

"We must be through the worst of the mountains," said Greg, rubbing his hands vigorously against Dathir. "The mountains ahead of us are much lower. Now we can thaw out!"

"Yes!" agreed Dathir. "As we came down I did not see anything nearly as high as the ones behind us. If only we could see the smoking mountain or the crater you described!"

"Have you any idea how far it might be from the pass?" Lyn asked.

"No. The tales do not say how far the dragons lived from the pass, yet it could not have been very far since they knew about it. Also we do not know in what direction they first fled."

"Aren't there any other clues?" questioned Lyn.

"No, the mountains and valley were never described."

"What about the direction of the wind?" Greg cried excitedly.

They were on the ground changing the carrying pad from Dathir to Lorimon when Greg said this, and Lorimon understood at once.

"You are right! They fled out of the path of the

smoke. See how all the branches bend towards the south? This means the prevailing winds are from the north, so we must head in that direction."

"Unless the wind was from another quarter the day of the explosion," said Greg, turning pessimistic.

"We shall find out," replied Dathir with a snort.

The dragons flew steadily all the rest of the day. In the morning, Lorimon had told Greg to put his and Lyn's breakfast leftovers in their pouches so they could eat while flying. Greg had forgotten to do this, and instead had put them in the basket. Since the children knew the dragons did not want to stop because there was so little time left, they said nothing about Greg's mistake and grew hungrier and hungrier.

"We shall fly until nightfall and then we shall eat," said Lorimon.

"But what?" asked Lyn. "There aren't enough leftovers, and it will be too dark for you to hunt."

Lorimon chuckled. "You are hungry." He doesn't know *how* hungry, Lyn thought to herself. "So are we. Before it grows too dark to see, Dathir will find something for us. There is plenty of game in the woods and fields below us. I have seen it."

It was close to sunset when they reached the end of the valley where the mountains were low and dipped down into several wide passes. As they flew through the nearest one, the dragons exclaimed together and paused, beating their great wings in place. In front of them, in the center of a small valley, a thin column of smoke poured out steadily from a low, solitary mountain with a truncated top.

No one spoke for a long moment. Then Lorimon said softly to his brother, "So! We have found it, after all our childhood imaginings and plannings!"

Dathir, who was given to doing acrobatics, flipped over a couple of times. "What a tale we shall have to tell when we return!" he cried out exultantly.

"I am glad we happen to be on Lorimon. I think Dathir would have forgotten we were on his back, in his jubilation!" Lyn whispered to Greg, who agreed wholeheartedly.

"Yes, much as I like Dathir, I always feel safer on Lorimon."

Dathir sped toward the mountain, calling over his shoulder, "Come swiftly! There is just time to see 'Smoketop' before it gets too dark."

"Keep out of the wind," Lorimon called back as they swept along. "Though probably there is no danger since the smoke is so thin and is mounting straight up."

They took a couple of wide sweeps around the crater with Greg and Lyn describing what little they knew about the inner workings of volcanoes. Afterwards they dropped down beside a small river.

"I suppose we'll have to do without dinner," said Lyn, trying to sound unconcerned.

"Not if I can help it," said Dathir and off he went.

He returned shortly with a fat deer, saying, "I saw it settling down to sleep in the tall grass and marked the place."

There was plenty of easily collected firewood and soon they gathered around a pleasant fire and jubilantly feasted on roast venison. Everyone was excited and even the dragons' silences were much shorter than usual.

The evening was spent discussing the best way to search for signs of the long-dead dragons.

"We can give two days to searching and still return on time if every day we start very early and fly until late," Lorimon decided.

" 'Smoketop' stands by itself in the center of this valley; if only we knew for certain which side the dragons lived on, our search would be easier," said Dathir.

Lyn clapped her hands excitedly. "I think I know! Isn't the crater slightly tipped away from us towards the other side? That means the main force of the explosion and therefore most of the lava poured down onto the part of the valley below it, and that is why the dragons' homes were so swiftly engulfed. If the crater had been tilted toward this side, perhaps most of the dragons would have had time to escape."

"Lyn's right," said Greg. "We must concentrate on the other side."

But a long day of searching brought no sign of the former or present dragons. The once-devestated valley had become green and fertile again. Flowers dotted the grass, and the trees were tall and majestic. The dragons were terribly disappointed.

"How can we be certain this is the right mountain unless we find some evidence of dragons having lived here?" Lorimon said. "And after tomorrow we must return."

It was Greg who, the next day, found what they were searching for. He wanted a piece of lava to take back to Earth, and so Lorimon landed on the sunny slope of one of the several hills that dotted the valley where an outcropping of long-cooled lava could be seen. Hundreds of tiny tendrils of vines had crept between the cracks and through the years had split the lava into many pieces. When Greg put his hands on each side of a chunk and pulled, a large slab fell off.

"What is that?" said Lyn curiously, staring at the exposed rock.

Lorimon gave a startled exclamation. "It is the remains of a dragon's egg! See, it is embedded in the lava!" He looked around. "Yes, this is just the type of place a dragoness would have picked in the days before we had nurseries – a warm, southern slope. Now we know we have found the place! Dathir! Dathir!" he called jubilantly as he shot up into the air. Dathir, who was searching farther away, was with them in a moment. He was even more exultant than his brother.

"We have succeeded! Now I cannot wait to get back and tell my friends, who thought we were wasting our leave!"

Then he quieted down and stood looking at the remains of the lava-bound egg, and when he spoke again he sounded sad. "Yet it grieves me to think of that child that was never born and of the parents. Were they also buried beneath the burning stone?

Or did they live to sorrow over the little one they never had?"

"There certainly are two sides to Dathir," Greg whispered to Lyn.

"Yes, and I wonder which one will win out in the end," Lyn answered thoughtfully.

They had a feast that night in a hollow near the crest of a hill that was not far from 'Smoketop'.

"Tomorrow," Lorimon said to the children, "we will start very early and fly steadily. So sleep well tonight and be sure a small gourd is filled with left-over food so that you can eat as we fly. By taking a shorter way, we hope to be able to cross the high pass tomorrow, and after that we will make good time."

A strong wind had sprung up and in the brilliant moonlight the speeding clouds shone very white. As Greg took a last look at 'Smoketop', a cloud drifted behind the mountain and its plume of smoke showed up clearly.

"There is much more smoke coming out of that crater than there was this morning," he said uneasily.

Both dragons had noticed it. "We have camped here because the wind is blowing away from us towards 'Smoketop'. See against the clouds how it is curved strongly in the other direction," said Dathir. "Now go to sleep, and be ready to leave at the first graying of the sky."

The dragons curved around them and the children, as usual, were asleep in a moment.

CHAPTER 4
Beyond the High Pass

"Wake up! Wake up!" Lyn drowsily heard Lorimon's voice and felt his head tapping her urgently. Vaguely she heard Dathir calling Greg. Feeling half-stupified, she managed to open her eyes and at once began coughing.

"Lorimon, don't blow your smoke in my face," she gasped crossly.

He kept shoving her with his head. "Haste, haste, the wind has changed and the smoke from the mountain is upon us!" She staggered to her feet. All around was acrid darkness; even the embers of their dying campfire gleamed through a dark haze.

"On my back, quickly!" urged Lorimon.

"Greg! Greg!" she shouted, choking as she did so.

"I'm on Dathir," he called back, ending in a cough.

Lyn scrambled onto Lorimon. He, too, was coughing as he took off. "Keep by me, Dathir," he called, "so we do not become separated. The smoke grows thinner in this direction."

He leapt up, driving forward. The pad had been left behind, and Lyn desperately tried to hold on with one hand while covering her nose and mouth with the fur mantle she found she was still clutching. Lorimon, however, was climbing so steeply in order to clear the trees swiftly that she was afraid she would fall off. So she dropped the mantle on his neck and laid her face against it. In this way she could hang on with both hands.

She heard him gasping long, harsh breaths, and twice felt his wings falter. Then the smoke lessened and they were suddenly out in the fresh air and clear skies, with only a few last wisps of smoke around them. Lyn drew in deep, thankful breaths, but felt too sick to lift her head. Lorimon was flying with great heaving breaths and his wingbeats were slow and unsteady. They were low, very low, barely skimming the treetops. Through half-closed eyes she was relieved to see Greg nearby, lying flat on Dathir, who was also flying unsteadily. A short distance further, the dragons glided down and collapsed beside a clump of trees, and lay there panting, not even bothering to fold their wings properly.

Lyn slid off onto the grass in a heap and lay there gasping until she heard Greg calling anxiously, "Where are you, Lyn? Are you all right?" She realized she was lying flat, right behind Lorimon, and so he could not see her. She sat up and called back, "I'm all right. How are you?"

He staggered around Lorimon and flopped down beside her. They lay there taking long, deep breaths and rejoicing in the clear air that filled their lungs. The sky was growing light when Greg at last got up and took a few shaky steps. "Whew, that was a close call!" he exclaimed.

Lyn also managed to stand up though she was

dizzy and coughed frequently. So did Greg.

"Look at Lorimon and Dathir," Lyn said in dismay. They were still lying with eyes and wings half-closed, and were panting in long, rasping breaths. Lyn caught her brother's arm. "Isn't there something we can do to help them? Suppose they don't recover! How would we ever get back?"

For a moment Greg looked as frightened as she felt. Then he said, "Perhaps water might help them. I think I glimpsed water gleaming as we came down, but I am not sure in which direction."

Still feeling very wobbly, they walked a little way from the trees up a slight incline. Greg had been right. There was a lovely lake that was fed by a small waterfall on one side and ended in a brook that rushed off in white-topped cascades down a steep slope and into another and much lower lake.

Lyn's feeble hooray was choked off by a cough. They stumbled down to the lake and splashed cold water on their faces, which partly revived them. Their mouths, though, felt dry and bitter no matter how many times they rinsed them out.

"I hope this horrible taste wears off soon," said Lyn, making a face. "It is all inside me, and the smell is all over me."

"I suppose it will take some days," said Greg. "Ugh, it's frightful! Now let's try to help Lorimon and Dathir. Luckily, Dathir slept with the utensils around his neck so they weren't lost. I was clinging to the rope that holds them."

They still felt weak and getting the rope off that held the utensils was no easy task, as it was impossible to get Dathir to lift his head even slightly. Finally, by standing on either side of his neck and pulling, they were able to work the rope first up his neck and then over his head. One last tug and it slipped. They tumbled down, panting. After resting a moment, they went down to the lake again, and each filled a large gourd. Then they came back and poured the cold water over the dragons' heads.

"It doesn't seem to help them," Lyn said anxiously.

"Let's get some more. They are so much bigger than we are, that undoubtedly they need more. Just watch." Greg spoke hopefully, to cheer himself as much as Lyn. Suppose the dragons *did* die? He forced the thought out of his head and filled his container again. Back and forth they went, pouring gourdful after gourdful over the dragons' heads. To their immense relief, after about the tenth dousing, Lorimon closed his eyes fully, settled his wings properly by his sides and took a deep breath. Dathir did the same a couple of drenchings later. That was better than their terrible, rasping gasps. Greatly relieved, the twins went back and forth several more times. At last, Lorimon lifted his head a little, shook it and opened his eyes. Then he rolled over onto his stomach.

"That is enough," he said with a faint chuckle, "or I shall be drowned. Now a drink would help." He drank several gourdfuls. "How is Dathir?"

Dathir was just coming around and he too wanted a drink. Both dragons were terribly weak and ill. They dragged themselves into the trees and lay there without speaking for hours.

The children followed them, exhausted by their efforts to revive them, and sat down. "We shall take turns keeping watch," Greg mumbled as he leaned comfortably against the warmth of Dathir's body.

"I suppose so," Lyn agreed drowsily.

It was late afternoon when she awoke. She stood up and was relieved to find that the giddiness was gone. She could walk around steadily and was beginning to feel hungry. There was enough food in the gourds for several small meals for humans, but not for dragons.

Greg was now awake and was also hungry. They ate a little, though not as much as they wanted.

"We must make our provisions last. And Dathir and Lorimon will be wanting food," Greg said.

"I wonder how long it will take them to recover? They had to inhale much more of the fumes than we did, because they were flying us."

"They'll be weak for days and won't be able to hunt. How shall we ever feed them?" said Greg.

"We can fish. I saw a good-sized one jump when we were carrying the water. Do you still have the fishhooks and lines?"

There was an anxious moment while Greg searched. "Here they are, I had forgotten I put them at the bottom of a gourd so that they would not fall out. Tomorrow we'll try our luck fishing."

The next morning the dragons were better but still weak and ill, and neither said more than a few words or wanted anything to eat. "Which is a good thing," commented Greg, "because we don't have anything yet. Let's start fishing."

"Wouldn't some of the herb soup the Healers taught you to make for the sick be better for them?"

"Of course, how stupid of me not to have thought of that!"

He searched carefully and came back with an armful of herbs and roots. In the meantime Lyn had collected what dry branches and twigs she could find, which took some time because they were not plentiful.

"How are we going to light it?" Greg asked. "We will have to wait until Lorimon or Dathir wakes up. I hope their flames haven't been affected by their being ill."

"No, they haven't. I will light it for you," said Lorimon who had overheard them. He pulled himself up, leaned forward and did so, then lay down and closed his eyes again.

The gourds, full of water and the herbs and roots which Greg had chopped up with his knife, were soon steaming invitingly. The pungent odor of the simmering soup roused the lethargic dragons, but neither were hungry.

"Do eat a little," Lyn coaxed Lorimon. "You know it will do you good."

"Yes, I know I should," Lorimon agreed reluctantly in answer to Lyn's urgings, and he did drink a gourdful, though very slowly.

No coaxing could persuade Dathir to eat. He refused, saying crossly, "I shall eat when I feel like it."

The next morning Lorimon was much better.

Dathir was still moody until Lorimon badgered him into drinking Greg's soup. After that, he regained his good spirits and apologized for his crossness.

"When Dathir is cross, he sometimes becomes so stubborn that he will not do what he knows he ought to do," Lorimon said privately to Lyn. She sympathized with Dathir.

"I know just how he feels. I'm that way, too, and so is Greg. Then we both get into trouble!"

Since the provisions were gone, the twins spent the morning fishing. They walked slowly along the edge of the lake, each with a line. They had no bait and it was a poor time of day for fishing, but the fish were unwary and struck at the bare hook, so they returned with a good catch. Greg cleaned the fish, which Lyn frankly admitted she hated doing, and wrapped them in damp, fragrant leaves. That evening the four of them had roasted fish.

The dragons, though greatly recovered, were still languid. Greg wondered at the effect the smoke had had on the naturally fire-breathing dragons.

"Was the volcano smoke so much worse than dragon smoke? When you fight, you are sometimes so surrounded with smoke that we on the ground can't see you. Or is it only dragon smoke you don't mind?"

"Dragon smoke, fire smoke, make no difference to us," Lorimon told them. "But there was death in that smoke, just as King Tolmar said. Did you not smell it? It burned my lungs and so filled them that I almost could not breathe and did not think I could get out of it before I fell."

"Nor did I," nodded Dathir, who had completely regained his good humor. "I could not see. My eyes were burning with the bitter smoke. I flew following Lorimon's wingbeats."

"Knowing that I had to get you to safety gave me the last bit of strength to get through," Lorimon continued, tapping Lyn gently with his head.

"Perhaps you would have gotten through quicker and with less ill effects if both of you had not had our added weight," she said.

Lorimon shook his head. "No. One can often get the strength to do for a friend what one cannot do for oneself."

Three days later, the dragons were recovered enough to start.

"At first we will fly slowly and rest frequently. By the third day we should have our full strength back," said Lorimon. "After that, we will, as I told you, start very early each morning and fly until late, because we will have overstayed our leave by several days and our uncle will be worried."

"Will you get in trouble because of that?" asked Lyn. She thought that would be terribly unfair since they had been so ill.

"No, of course not," said Lorimon looking at them in astonishment, "since we did not overstay our leave deliberately; but the King will guess that some accident has befallen us and he will be anxious."

"Will he send out a search party?" Greg queried.

"Perhaps, but they will not know where to search for us. All anyone knows, and all we ourselves knew when we started, was that we were going to keep heading north."

"Anyway, our uncle would undoubtedly wait several days to see if we had been delayed merely by a bad storm," said Dathir as he chuckled delightedly. "It will be fun to have a real reason for overstaying one's leave!"

Lorimon chuckled also. "Dathir likes to drop into his post at the last possible moment."

"I have never been late, have I?" Dathir retorted. "Lorimon, on the contrary, returns so far ahead of time that he is asleep by the time I am beginning to think of going back!"

Both brothers laughed. Lorimon leaned over and swung his head against Dathir's neck and engaged in what Lyn, who had often seen dragons do it before, called "a friendly head-wrestling match". They sparred for a few moments.

"Now I am certain we are well enough to fly back," said Lorimon, settling down again, "and keep up a good speed, too."

"We won't be able to hang on if you go fast, since we no longer have the pad," Lyn pointed out, privately doubting if she could hang on for one long day, even if they went slowly.

"Wait a minute," said Dathir. He leapt into the air and came down again after searching the sky with a quick, circular glance. "The wind is blowing the smoke directly away from us. I remember where we were that night and will get your pad." He flew off.

"Do go along and keep an eye on him," Lyn

begged Lorimon. "He might do something foolish, such as going close to the volcano just for the sake of the danger or of being able to say that he did."

Lorimon glanced at her sharply. "I see you understand my brother. You are correct in one way. Dathir does enjoy showing off, and he likes to flirt with danger. But he is no fool. He knows that mountain holds death and will not go nearer to it than necessary."

Lorimon had not been mistaken. Dathir was soon back with the pad.

"Originally we had planned to fly back to the high pass by the shortest route, but that would take us over the higher mountains and neither of us wish to tackle them the first day. They are much lower in the west, so we will fly that way and cross them more easily," said Lorimon as they started off the next morning.

The first day's journey was a pleasant one for the children. Not only did the dragons rest frequently, but the rests were fairly long and they had plenty of time to look around. "And," said Lyn when they stopped near a lovely, small waterfall, "just to lie in the grass and enjoy the scenery."

The next morning the dragons flew more strongly and rested less. In the early afternoon the sky clouded over and such a heavy cloudburst poured down that Lorimon and Dathir reluctantly came down near a small pond and took shelter in the thick woods that grew almost to its margin.

Like most cloudbursts, the rain was soon over and the dragons prepared to resume their flight.

Greg was disappointed because he had hoped to go fishing, and urged them to camp there for the night since there was water and plenty of firewood.

While they were discussing this, Lyn, who was sitting at the edge of the woods admiring a rainbow, cried out, "Look! There's a dragon!"

She expected Lorimon and Dathir to leap upwards at once, calling out a welcome, but instead they crept forward cautiously and peered out.

"Keep back under the trees," Lorimon ordered. "Do not let yourselves be seen."

"But why? You've been looking for dragons and here is one," Greg protested.

"Certainly we have been looking for dragons. But are they expecting us? And will they take us as friends . . . or captives?" Dathir said grimly.

Long before Lyn could see anything more than that the dragon was heading towards the pond, Lorimon exclaimed, "It is a Green Dragoness!"

The dragons pulled back until they and the children were completely hidden by the bushes, and waited.

The dragoness alighted and began to fill one of the two large gourds she was carrying. She was quite close and they could see she was weeping. As she picked up the second gourd to fill it, Lorimon slipped quietly forward and said, "Greetings, Lady, in the name of the Great One. Do not fear us, I beg you."

The dragoness whirled around, her wings half-opened, ready for sudden flight. Then she paused, staring at him in amazement. Lorimon made no further move towards her.

"Who are you?" she asked. She did not sound frightened, only surprised.

"Lady," replied Lorimon, "I am Lorimon, and my brother Dathir is with me. We are descendants of those dragons who, long generations ago, fled with King Tolmar when 'Smoketop' blew up and destroyed the valley with fire and deadly smoke. They fled southward, ever southward, until they came to that land by the sea where we now dwell, and there he established his kingdom."

Dathir had now come forward, and the dragoness looked at them intently. Then she said slowly, "You greeted me in the name of the Great One. Did you mean that truly?"

"Of course we mean it," Lorimon said in surprise. He then said curiously, "Why do you ask me that?"

"The name of the Great One is used freely here, and not always well."

"Then they are not true Green Dragons," said Lorimon indignantly. "When we are given the gold armband do you think we swear empty promises?"

The dragoness looked bewildered. "What do you mean? I know well the tale of how in the reign of King Tolmar, fire from 'Smoketop' devastated the valley where the Green Dragons had lived for so long. We, too, are descended from those who escaped and later settled here, but I have never heard anything about gold armbands, though I see that you both wear one."

"Forgive me, Lady. In my astonishment I forgot

65

that the wearing of the gold armband as a pledge of keeping the laws of the Great One started only with the coming of the Master of Wisdom."

Lorimon then told her about the Master of Wisdom, and the pledge every young dragon and dragoness makes to keep the laws of the Great One. Lyn had never heard him speak so movingly and earnestly. When he finished explaining about the Blue Road, the dragoness came closer, her eyes shining.

"How I wish I lived among those who truly obey the laws of the Great One, and oh, that I might see the Blue Road!" Her voice was pathetic with longing.

"Lady," said Lorimon gently. "Return with us. The King is our uncle, and I know he will welcome you and give you a place to live."

"If only I could!" she cried out earnestly. "But I have a grandfather and a young brother. How could I leave them behind?"

"They can come with us if they also sincerely wish to live by our laws."

"They do. Yet how could we escape? My grandfather flies well, but after all, he is old; and my brother is, as I said, young."

"Escape!" exclaimed Dathir. "Would you be kept here against your will?"

"Yes. They would seem to allow us to leave, so that our Chief would appear to be just and magnanimous. Then you two would be slain for some 'good' reason or other. Some of us have often spoken of leaving, but had no one to guide us, and we also knew that pursuit would be swift . . . and deadly." The dragoness' eyes filled with tears and she began to weep again.

"I have never heard of anything like this!" Dathir exclaimed contemptuously. "They claim to hold the truths we do, but their actions smack more of those of the Dark Dragons! Though truly, in this I think the Dark Dragons are more honest – they do not pretend. To think that I am speaking well of the Dark Dragons!" he ended, muttering to himself.

Lorimon spoke even more gently than before. "Lady, you were weeping when we first saw you. Can you not tell us your sorrow?"

"The son of our Chief wishes to marry me and I detest him. He says he follows the Great One – as everyone here claims to do! – and would marry me according to our age-old customs; but he would not be faithful for any longer than he chose to be . . . which would not be long."

"Are you not free to refuse him? In our land everyone may choose to marry whom they please."

"Supposedly it is the same here. In his fair words and promises, though, are veiled threats to my young brother. Were it only threats to myself, I would not care," said the dragoness scornfully, tossing her head with a proud gesture. "He could kill me before I would accept him; it is my brother I fear for. I have put off this dragon several times. This morning he returned, and his threats were no longer veiled. If I do not consent, his father would command my brother to serve him and then . . . 'well, unfortunately, accidents do happen'. Those were his actual words."

"How dare they call themselves Green Dragons!" Lorimon exploded. He and Dathir were breathing out small flames. "Lady, you must flee with us."

"My name is Alamirna. Do you think there is any hope of our reaching your land safely? Yet, somehow, you give me hope," she added in a low voice. "Surely you were meant to find and help us."

At this point Lyn and Greg, who had remained hidden, moved forward so as to see and hear better. Alamirna saw them and gasped. "What are they?"

Lorimon chuckled and introduced them. "They are our companions and faithful friends, and have been friends of the Green Dragons for many, many passings. Let them tell you their own tale."

"Wait. Here we can easily be seen. Under the trees we shall be hidden from spying eyes above," said Dathir.

The dragoness listened with growing amazement to all that Lyn and Greg told her. Then she asked Lorimon and Dathir many questions about the Green Dragons, the Master, and above all about the Blue Road.

"We will flee with you, my grandfather, my brother and I, and if we fall by the way, so be it. We shall have done the right thing, and I know I would always regret not having tried."

She thanked them all, especially Lorimon who had done most of the talking.

"Lady," he replied, "it is I who must thank you, for in explaining these things to you, I have learned to value them still more."

CHAPTER 5
The L-shaped Valley

Dusk was falling. "I shall go now. Wait for me here," Alamirna said. She started out from the woods, then called softly over her shoulder, "A dragon is coming! Remain hidden. I will let you know whether he is a friend or an enemy."

She picked up her second gourd and filled it without looking upwards. A dragon dropped down beside her, bowed his head and tried to lay it against hers. She drew it away sharply.

"Alamirna, my beloved, when do I get my answer?" said the dragon. "You have kept me waiting so long."

"When I please!" retorted the dragoness.

"Come now, I wish it soon!" He moved closer to her. She again moved away from him. When he saw this, an angry note came into his voice. "I want an answer and I want it soon . . . or else your brother starts service with my father!"

With a coquettish twist of her head, she glanced at him. "Leave me in peace for two days, and on the third I will answer you."

He was at her side in a moment. "Why not now?"

She picked up the gourds and slung them around her neck, giving him another coquettish nod as she did so. "Because a dragoness has a right to keep her suitor waiting a while." She flew off.

The dragon gave a nasty chuckle and called after her, "Very well, on the third morning I shall be expecting your consent," and he too flew off.

"She is a valiant dragoness and we must save her," said Lorimon. "How I longed to engage that 'son of their chief' in combat! How dare he threaten her like that!"

"So did I," agreed Dathir. "I could barely restrain myself."

"How are you going to save her, and her grandfather and brother?" asked Greg. "There are only two of you."

"And," the words came out before Lyn could stop them, "if anything happens to you, what will become of us? We can't walk back."

"We have two days," replied Lorimon. "Did you not hear how cleverly she put him off?"

"Yes. In two days we can be far away," said Dathir. "If only we were certain just how far the high pass is from here. We know its general whereabouts," he continued, seeing Greg's surprised expression, "and could find it easily enough with a little searching. But there will be no time for searching now. We shall have to fly as fast as we can."

"Which means as fast as the slowest among us, which will either be her grandfather or her brother," added Lorimon.

"Or how well we can hang on. I know you have never flown anywhere near as fast as you can when

70

carrying us, but now you will have to," said Lyn, thinking what it would be like to be blown about by wind that was coming from their great wings which would be beating as swiftly as they could. "Then, too, what would happen should you have to fight?"

Dragons always face their problems straight on, and never pretend that they are not there.

"You are right," said Lorimon. "Yet it seems to me that, as Alamirna said, we were sent to help these few far-off relatives of ours who have held fast to what is right when others have not, even though in coming we had no thought of such a thing. See how we were driven here by the smoking mountain!"

"The old Master we knew before always said there was no such thing as chance," said Greg thoughtfully. "He said everything fitted, piece by piece, into one great pattern which we might see and understand here and there, but never completely until we were beyond the Blue Road."

"Yes, that is what we are taught from childhood, and therefore each one must do their piece to the best of their ability," responded Lorimon.

"For you it must be hard, as you do not wear the armband. But for us it is not difficult," Dathir said, a trifle complacently, Lyn thought. "But come, let us sleep; we have to fly far tonight."

"I wish you would not think it so easy to do well, my brother," said Lorimon quietly. Dathir ignored the remark and was quickly asleep. "He is right; we must sleep," added Lorimon and curled up also.

At first the children were too excited to think of sleeping and were finally just dozing off when a half-grown dragon dropped down calling softly, "Lorimon, Dathir; I have come from Alamirna, my sister."

The dragons crept quickly to the edge of the trees.

"What is your message?" asked Lorimon.

"We are ready to leave whenever you tell us to. Shall we come here or do you wish to meet us where we live? It is not far and we live apart from the others, except for one young couple. They, too, wish to flee."

"Your sister told them about our coming?" Dathir asked in surprise. "I did not think she would be so foolish as to risk this venture by telling others."

"My sister did not risk this venture," said the young dragon loyally. "Yet how could we leave this pair behind when they, too, long to serve the Great One truly? You do not know how often they have spoken with us of fleeing." He hesitated a moment before continuing. "I know, though she thinks I do not, that the only reason my sister would agree to marrying the Chief's son is to save me. Rather than bring such unhappiness upon her, I was planning to leave secretly."

"Well spoken, young one," said Lorimon approvingly. "You have a brave heart like your sister. It is dark enough for us not to be seen. Are there trees near where you live, under which we could conceal ourselves? I would like to see one of your homes."

"There are trees all around. Follow me. They are waiting."

Lorimon slipped on the pad and warned Lyn and Greg to lie as flat as they could along his back. "If you sat upright, your outlines would seem so strange to anyone who saw them, that we would be investigated at once out of sheer curiosity, if for no other reason."

Greg got into the front position and lay flat, and Lyn crouched behind him, while the dragons flew so low that the treetops brushed against their legs.

Alamirna's brother landed first, then flew up at once calling softly that all was safe and they could come down. They did, and found Alamirna, her grandfather, and a young couple with a baby waiting and pretending to be chatting sociably.

Lorimon and Dathir questioned them closely and were soon satisfied that they were sincere in their desire to leave and willing to risk their lives in the attempt.

"There are a few others," said the young husband with a sigh, "that I think would gladly come with us, yet we cannot risk telling them as they live where they would be seen if they left."

Alamirna had a good dinner ready. "We others have eaten while waiting. Now you must eat as well." From their hiding place under the trees they could look into Alamirna's home, which was a cave. It was spacious and there were plenty of gourds, and hides piled up for beds, but it was poor-looking in comparison with the dragon houses they knew.

"What will they think when they see our dragons' houses and the palace?" Lyn whispered to Greg.

"I don't know, but I certainly admire them for giving up what is everything to them and facing the unknown. They don't know how much more they will have in the end."

"A hundredfold more," Lyn said softly.

"Yes. Now let's hope we get back safely."

Lorimon and Dathir ate only lightly. "Your meal is delicious, Lady," Lorimon said approvingly as he and Dathir thanked her. "If we do not eat heartily it is because we have far to fly and must leave soon. We came into this land over a very high pass to the south of where we are. Do any of you know exactly where it is?"

"We all know where it is," replied the grandfather. "Some of the more adventurous among us occasionally fly through it, as I did in my younger days, but it is high and cold even for us who are accustomed to mountain heights. We have often discussed whether we should try that way when we talked together about leaving this place. It is a long time since I was there, but I can easily find it."

"I know it also," said the young husband, whose name was Malthor. "It is only a day's steady flight from here if we flew straight towards it, but that would not be wise as we would have to pass directly over the most populated part of this valley. I think it would be wiser to fly first around the lower mountains and then head towards the pass. The hunting is poor as the last stretch of the valley before the pass is rather barren, so few ever go there."

After a brief discussion Lorimon and Dathir agreed that this was the best plan.

"We will wait a little longer until the moon has set and then leave. Are there guards posted in the valley?" Lorimon asked.

"Guards!" exclaimed Alamirna. "No. Why should we have guards? You are the first strangers we have ever seen."

"No watchers set to give warning should there be a fire or another 'Smoketop' blowing up? Hmm," said Dathir disapprovingly. "Your dragons cannot be warriors, though in this case it is well for us."

While they waited, the mother wrapped her baby warmly in a soft skin. "How will you carry it?" Lyn asked. "Don't you have a carrying basket?"

"What is a carrying basket? I will carry him close to me. That is our way."

"That might be all right for carrying him about in the valley, but won't you get tired carrying him all day?"

"My husband will help me when I am tired."

The mother was, however, very impressed when Lyn showed her their basket. Lyn emptied it out and the mother put her baby in it, but he was terrified at being confined and wailed and thrashed about so much, that he had to be taken out before he hurt himself.

"I think I can help you," said Greg. He knew how to make all sorts of sailor knots and in a few moments he had the baby firmly trussed up like a package, with only its little nose sticking out from the soft, warm skin. Next he made a harness that went around the mother's neck.

She was delighted. "Now he will be safe and I can fly with more ease."

Telling the children that he had to be free in case of an attack, Lorimon transferred their carrying pad to Alamirna, which made Lyn nervous, though she saw that the dragoness listened carefully to his instructions.

Alamirna must have guessed her fears, because just before they took off, she said, "I am very privileged to be carrying you, though I know you will miss your friends. I will try to fly as smoothly as I can and you must tell me if I go too fast or rise or drop too steeply."

Lorimon gave final instructions. "Fly low and spread out until each can just hear a wingbeat on each side. Do not speak. Head towards the peak we agreed on. You, Malthor, lead us. At the first graying of the sky we must all come together and drop down to rest in some place where we can be hidden. You set the wingbeat, Alamirna, as you know best what speed your grandfather and brother can maintain. Let us go, and may the Great One be with us." And up he leapt.

It was strange to be on an unknown dragoness, even though she flew very smoothly, so smoothly that Lyn who was in front and lying flat began to doze off, lulled by the regular beat of her wings. Greg felt her slipping and shook her awake.

"Pinch yourself," he said urgently, forgetting

that she was hanging on with both hands. "Bite your tongue, do anything to keep yourself awake."

He soon needed the same advice himself as he too began to doze. He pulled himself up and whispered to Lyn that surely they could sit up as it was so dark he could barely see Alamirna's head. That was better, and the chill wind helped to keep them awake for a while, but both were nodding when the small band came together early in the morning and, led by Malthor, landed in a wooded spot near a stream.

"I will keep watch," he said. "As I told you, this is not a good place for hunting, but for one it is not bad and I sometimes hunt around here. Everyone knows that and so no one will be suspicious if they see me."

They remained there until noon when the northern dragons, Alamirna assured Lorimon, were resting.

"That is good," he said. "We can fly farther."

They did for a while and then rested again until dusk, when they took off again. Lorimon allowed them only one brief pause around midnight.

Lyn and Greg promptly fell asleep, warmed by Alamirna and each other. In what seemed like just a few minutes, Alamirna woke them. "Lorimon has ordered us to start flying again." There was no use grumbling, so they wearily climbed on again.

Towards dawn Malthor said, "We are coming to the high pass." They had been flying along the base of high mountains and as they came around a shoulder that projected well into the plain, they saw it. It loomed far above them, looking cold and white and dangerous, between the twin peaks of sheer ice.

"It makes me shudder even to look at it," Lyn said to her brother.

"We have been through it once, we can go through it again," said Dathir. "It is our pursuers, if there are any, who are the greatest danger."

"But haven't we made good time?" Greg asked in surprise.

Dathir shook his head. "No, we are flying slowly but cannot go faster. Dragons in their prime could easily catch up with us. However, if Alamirna's words have really won us two days, then I think we are safe."

"You are right, though, Lyn," said Lorimon. "The high pass is a danger. We must go through it as soon as everyone is rested, even before the sun is fully upon it. At this time we must attempt it even if a cold wind is blowing, as we do not dare to remain here. It will be harder for you than for us. You remember how nearly frozen you were even though we had waited until the wind had died down."

"Don't worry about us," said Lyn, trying to laugh; she remembered only too well how bitterly cold the pass had been. "If Alamirna will just blow out a few flames before she starts climbing to the pass, she will be so hot that if we lie flat against her we will be warm."

"You have no idea, Lorimon, how much you dragons heat up when you breathe out flame. The last time we were here, King Damor – he was still a prince then – once was terribly angry and got so hot that our legs were nearly scorched!" Greg added.

While they waited, Lyn kept looking up at the pass. She did not want to, but its height drew her eyes like a magnet and she shivered every time she saw it. She had forgotten how much lower the valley was on this side than on the other, and even the thought of the steep climb that would be necessary to reach it, made her dizzy. If only Lorimon was going to be carrying them, she would not mind it quite so much, she thought, as she craned her neck backwards to see the pass. As she watched, a cloud floated through it and she tried to shove out of her mind the realization of how wet and freezingly cold they would be if they flew through a wet cloud. She had a vivid imagination, and she could see Greg and herself being frozen solid.

The wind showed no signs of abating and soon Lorimon said, "Well, we must attempt the high pass whether the wind is blowing or not."

He gave precise directions. All were to fly through as fast as they could without pausing and drop down to the small plateau below the pass and there wait until all were through. He told Dathir to lead the way, followed by the young couple. Alamirna would go next carrying the children, and then her brother and grandfather. He would bring up the rear.

"No," said the grandfather firmly. "I know I am the slowest and could endanger the passage if you wait for me. I shall go last. Either I shall make it or I shall not. If I do not, then go on without me. It is foolish to let one endanger all."

No amount of persuading could change his mind. "Here I remain," he said stubbornly, "until I see Lorimon heading through the pass. Now go, or else it will be too late."

They had to go. Because of the difficulty of breathing at that altitude, none of the dragons wished to fly upwards at a steep angle and so they flew out over the plain and headed towards the pass slowly and at a broad angle. This made hanging on much easier for the children, but it also meant they would be longer in the thin, freezing air. Alamirna heated herself up as they asked her to do and, though it was indeed far colder this time, Lyn found that at least half of her was warm, the half along Alamirna's back; but even that grew cold when they came into the pass. The freezing wind was so bitter she could barely breathe. Just as she wondered if she could stand it a moment longer, they were out of the pass and dropping slowly to the prearranged meeting place below in the short leg of the L-shaped valley. Alamirna's brother landed right behind them and Lorimon a moment after. There they all waited, staring anxiously at the pass for a sign of the old dragon.

For what seemed like ages, they watched. Then, with a great flapping of wings he came through and dropped heavily down. His sides were heaving.

"We are being pursued!" he panted. "Someone must have seen us leaving. They are still far behind, but there can be no doubt. They are heading for the pass."

"How many are there?" Dathir asked.

"They were too far away for me to see clearly, but at least ten."

"We shall have to fight. We have no choice," said Lorimon. "Dathir and I will try to hold them as long as we can, while the rest of you fly swiftly around the bend of this valley. If you can get to where the trees are dense before being seen, scatter widely and drop down and hide until night. Greg and Lyn will have to guide you back. Head south, always south, crossing the ranges by the lowest passes. May the Great One be with you."

Lyn's heart sank. She knew he was saying farewell. He and Dathir were undoubtedly far better warriors than the untrained northern dragons, but even so, they would fall, overwhelmed by numbers. He was beside her and, choking back her tears, she hugged him hastily.

"Farewell," he said gently. "Climb on Alamirna's back quickly."

"I will fight, too," said Malthor. "That will give them more time to escape."

"So will I," said the grandfather. "I could not help them on their flight. I would only hold them back."

"I will fight also," said Alamirna decidedly. "I would rather die than be led back a captive of that horrible dragon. You carry Lyn and Greg," she said to the young mother.

"No," commanded Lorimon. "Flee also with your brother. What use is it if we all fall? You must lead them."

81

"Lorimon is right," Malthor urgently said to his wife. "Flee at once."

For a few moments longer the dragonesses hesitated, then, Alamirna flew off the plateau crying to her brother, "Come! We must obey Lorimon's orders."

With a weeping farewell to her husband, the young mother followed, clasping her baby tightly.

As they went around the curve the children gave a last look back. The dragons were conferring on the plateau.

As soon as they were well into the long valley, Alamirna looked anxiously around for the best hiding place.

"See where the valley widens and the trees are very dense . . ." she was beginning, then cried out in alarm as two green dragons rose suddenly from the trees below them.

"Halt! Who goes there?" they called out.

Lyn screamed and then gasped as she saw both dragons wore the gold armband, and one also wore on his left arm the bronze band which was the insignia of the Captain of the Border Guard.

Greg recognized him at the same time. "Captain! Captain!" they shouted. Another dragon flew up. This one had a gold collar. It was the Prince.

"Lyn, Greg," he called anxiously, "where are Lorimon and Dathir?"

"Go and help them at once!" Greg yelled. "They are trying to hold back ten dragons who are pursuing us, so that we could escape! Right around the curve at the end of the valley!"

"Yes! Hurry! Hurry, or it will be too late!" shouted Lyn. "They are giving their lives to save us!"

The Captain barked a command and more warriors immediately flew up from where they had been resting, hidden among the trees. They were in formation and speeding up the valley before the startled dragonesses could begin to ask questions.

"Fly after them, please," begged Greg. "They're friends. The one with the gold collar is the Prince."

"And the Captain of the Border Guard is the one with the bronze armband. The rest are his warriors. They'll protect us," explained Lyn excitedly.

In a moment the dragonesses were following as fast as they could while the children shouted explanations as to who the dragons were. The dragonesses were no match for the warriors in speed, but they did not fall very far behind in the short distance back and they managed to reach the bend as the warriors swept up into combat position beside the four other dragons who had just engaged their pursuers. "Hooray! Hooray!" the children yelled as loudly as they could.

The fight was quickly over. The newcomers were not fighting to kill but were only trying to drive the northern dragons to the ground and, as they did so, called on them to surrender. One by one the northern dragons did and dropped down, except for one who was fighting fiercely with the Captain and getting the worst of it. He could be heard calling to another dragon who had already surrendered but had not yet dropped down, but the other dragon made no move to help him. The fight ended abruptly with the northern dragon falling downward. He hit the ledge of the plateau and with a loud cry flipped over and crashed into the trees far below. Then the other dragon dropped down and the Captain did also.

Heedless of any flapping wings which could easily have knocked them over, Lyn and Greg ran in among the dragons to greet the Prince and the others.

"Lorimon! Dathir! Are you badly hurt?" Lyn asked anxiously, seeing blood on both of them. They had been attacked by several dragons just before the warriors arrived and were wounded, but only slightly.

"No! They don't know the first points of combat," said Dathir contemptuously.

"How did you know we needed help so badly?" Lorimon exclaimed in amazement to the Prince. "A little later would have been too late!"

"The Master said to come. What was the reason for this fight?"

Lorimon quickly related to the Prince and Captain what had happened. "Alamirna says there are more who would return with us, but I had no authority to invite them. With these it was different. They were fleeing and I knew the King would be as indignant as we were that a young dragoness should be forced by threats into a marriage she detested," Lorimon ended vigorously.

"You were right," said the Prince. "Now I understand why the Master urged me to come. For some reason I was growing extremely anxious about all of you. More and more strongly I felt that you needed me. Finally I went to the Master and told him my fears. 'Go at once,' he told me, 'and take warriors with you.'

"My father was extremely reluctant to give me permission and wanted only the Captain to lead this band. The Master, however, said one would be needed who could make decisions for the realm, so at last my father let me go, and gave me full authority to act in his place. Who is your leader?" he asked, turning towards the captured dragons.

"He is the one who fell," answered one of them.

"I am his son, so I am the Chief now," said another.

The Captain looked at him with disgust. "You are the one to whom he called for help. You are his son, yet you did not move a wing to come to his rescue!"

"I saw he could not win, and why should both of us fall? Who would be left to be the leader?" the dragon replied unconcernedly.

The Green warriors looked in contempt at him and muttered among themselves. "He speaks like a Dark Dragon! And to think they are Green Dragons like ourselves! Let us return to our land and leave them to their evil ways."

Alamirna and her grandfather were talking earnestly with one of the northern dragons. He listened intently and then addressed Lorimon. "Is what she says true? That all of you really obey the laws of the Great One instead of just talking about them?"

"Yes, it is, or at least we really try to."

"Well, really trying is about all anyone can do," was the gruff reply. "But how do I know you are speaking the truth?"

"I swear by the Blue Road," Lorimon answered earnestly.

"There is no way of your knowing if we tell the truth or not except by trusting us," interposed the Prince quietly.

"True," said the gruff dragon, whose name was Radkar. He looked hard at Lorimon and the Prince for a long time and then said as though half speaking to himself, "The Blue Road. I have never heard of it, but something tells me you would not dare swear falsely by it." He looked straight at Lorimon. "My wife and I would like to live in your land if we have your leave to come with you."

"It is not for me to give any such permission," said Lorimon. "Only our King can do that. Here is his son, the Crown Prince, to whom the King has given authority to act in his name."

Lyn liked the look of the gruff dragon and hoped the Prince would let him come.

The grandfather added quickly, "He did not join in the attack."

"Why?" the Prince asked Radkar.

"The Old Chief told us, or at least me – he may have told some of the others the truth! – that we were pursuing strange dragons who were kidnappers. When I saw my old friend here, and Malthor, and only two strangers, I guessed at once what had happened and would have no part in the murder, for that is what it would have been if you had not arrived. Right then and there I made up my mind I would not remain here any longer, but would try to find the land where you came from."

"That is a brave speech, and you and your wife and children, if you have any, may live with us," said the Prince. "Are there many in your land who would want to return with us? The journey is a wearying one."

"Leaving the place and friends you have always known is hard. There are a few who will do so in order to live freely what they believe, or for the sake of the future of their children. Others might want to, but not enough to leave all behind."

"Very well, we shall go back to your land," said the Prince, "and then any who do wish to leave must speak to me. Captain, you take over now."

The Green warriors had stopped panting from their exertions in the unaccustomed thin air and were now eyeing the high pass in a rather unhappy manner. Not one, though, made the slightest gesture of refusal when told they were going to fly through it. Lorimon explained carefully the best way to attempt it. After he told them that he and Dathir had done it twice, and that the valley on the other side was much lower, they looked more cheerful.

The Captain divided his warriors. Half, with himself at the head, were to go first, followed by Lorimon. Next would come the prisoners and behind them the remaining warriors, the Prince, Dathir and the other dragons. The children were again on Alamirna.

"Those northern dragons are going to have a shock when they see us return," Greg said to Lyn.

"Nothing like the shock I had when the Captain shot up from the forest just when I thought all was lost!"

"Or mine when Lorimon said I would have to guide the escaping dragons back!" he rejoined with a laugh.

The return trip through the pass went easily; the wind had died down and the sun was shining full on it. Before Lyn had time to really be cold, they were through and gliding down into the warmer and thicker air. As soon as all were down, the Captain told a couple of warriors to take care of the wounded dragons. Lorimon's and Dathir's wounds were quickly eased. Malthor had two slight ones and Alamirna's grandfather had none.

"I do not think any of them would have deliberately wounded my grandfather, except perhaps the Chief," Alamirna said in explanation.

Several of the northern dragons also had wounds; three were serious though the dragons could still fly. When the gruff dragon, Radkar, saw the two warriors treating the northern dragons' wounds as carefully as they had Lorimon's and Dathir's, he grunted, "Now I know what you say is true."

CHAPTER 6
The Warriors' Return

On the way back to the Chief's realm, two of the prisoners – the new Chief was one of them – tried to escape but were surrounded and forced back. As soon as they were in the Chief's realm, the Prince ordered him to summon all his dragons. The Chief refused sulkily and so Alamirna and Radkar did the summoning while the Chief and his band were held on the ground under constant supervision.

When all were gathered, the Prince explained what was happening, and then asked if any wished to come with him. He put before them the hardships of the journey and what would be expected of them in their new country. The northern dragons were, as Greg had predicted, startled and apprehensive when they discovered their Chief and his strongest supporters were being held prisoner right in the middle of their own dwellings. It took some time before they could be persuaded they would not be injured, and that they were perfectly free to choose whether to stay or migrate to the south. The Captain had to explain several times that the Chief and the others were only being kept as hostages so that those who wished to leave could do so freely without being cowed by threats.

The assembled dragons conferred among themselves for a long time. Greg, who happened to overhear some of their remarks, said to Lorimon, "I suspect that quite a few of them are not sorry to see their Chief taken down a peg or two."

Lorimon laughed. "We say 'taken down a wing-beat or two.' I think you are right. I suspect that most of them find him overbearing."

The dragons asked many questions, even of Lyn and Greg. "We have never seen anything like you," one of them said, "but since you know this southern land yet do not belong to it, you will probably tell the truth."

"What the Prince tells you is true. Every word of it," Lyn insisted.

"These Green Dragons never lie," Greg added emphatically.

"Hmmm," said one of his listeners. "That is difficult to believe."

"Don't judge by what goes on here," Greg shouted indignantly. His audience merely chuckled and he felt terribly frustrated.

"Why can't they believe?" he said impatiently to Lyn.

"I think they just don't know how to," she said sadly, feeling as frustrated as he did.

The Prince gave the dragons until the next morning to make up their minds. "Go home and talk it over," he urged them.

The dragons did talk it over but none of them went back to their caves. "We have never seen other dragons than ourselves," they explained. "Now that we see that no one is going to get hurt or taken permanently prisoner, it is entertaining to have strangers to talk with." They even brought food for everyone.

"Besides, some of the dragons are very handsome," whispered one young dragoness to Lyn. "Do introduce me to your friend, Dathir. I have never seen anyone like him, so trim, so muscular, and just look at his eyes." She tossed her head flirtatiously. "I am certain we would get on well together."

Lyn did not introduce her to Dathir, but the dragoness managed to speak with him. Afterwards, each time he happened to be looking in her direction, she rolled her eyes at him.

The tough Radkar did not wait until the next morning to bring his wife, who was a quiet, kindly dragoness, to speak to the Prince. In answer to the Prince's questions and warnings, she said simply, "Yes, I know it will be difficult to change to other ways even though they are better than ours, but they *are* better and that is what is important. I also know that the journey will be hard, but with Radkar I would go anywhere."

Nor did another couple wait. They were youngsters, a dragon of thirty-two passings and his sister, a timid little thing of twenty-three. They came forward quickly as though afraid they might be forcibly stopped, and begged the Prince to allow them to come with him.

When the new Chief who was nearby heard them, he roared with anger and with a quick leap landed beside the little dragoness and beat her with his head. She cowered as though used to such treatment. The Chief did not strike her twice. The Captain was within what the dragons call "head distance" and struck him such a sharp blow with his head that the Chief recoiled.

"Never dare touch that child again," the Captain commanded angrily, while his warriors murmured indignantly.

"I am their guardian," said the Chief. "They cannot leave without my permission."

"He is nothing of the sort," said Radkar. "Their father was the old Chief's younger brother. The old Chief was jealous of him because he was popular, and I have always suspected that his death was no hunting accident. Their mother died two passings ago. The Chief kept these children to wait on him and, as you can see, beat them frequently. If you do not take them with you, the dragon will soon 'disappear', and his sister's life will be more miserable than ever."

The Captain called the children over. "You are now under my protection," he said. "If anyone dares to touch you, they will get a thrashing they will never forget." So that was happily settled, to the rage of the Chief.

Lyn giggled at the energetic way the Captain had solved the problem. "Doesn't the Chief look furious?" she said to Greg. "Can you imagine Alamirna having to be married to that beast?"

The Chief was indeed furious, as she found out later to her terror.

Since the prisoners were under close guard, she and Greg, without mentioning it to anyone, decided to stroll around and stretch their legs.

"Flying on a dragon is fun, but I am always so stiff at the end of the day. It's going to be a long trip and so I'm going to walk about while I can," said Lyn.

"That's too slow. I'm going to sprint," said Greg, and off he dashed, vaulting over a friendly tail here and there. Lyn walked briskly around the large circle of dragon guards a couple of times, and then walked back through the dragons without noticing how near she came to the Chief. With a sudden, vicious twitch of his wings, he knocked her over against another dragon who, with a nasty chuckle, knocked her back against the Chief who twitched again. Battered and terrified, she managed to scream, only to be knocked down again. Fortunately, Dathir was close by and with a couple of head thrusts, shoved the dragons apart. Bruised and shaken though uninjured, she stumbled to safety.

Dathir would have given the two dragons a sharp lesson, but was stopped by the Captain.

"We shall be gone by tomorrow. There is no use in making them angrier than they already are, or they may try some treachery." Then, after asking Lyn if she was hurt, he proceeded to scold her for having been very foolish. "I command you not to go near these captives again," he said brusquely. "Your brother has more sense than you have; he keeps near friends."

In spite of her bruises and shaking up, or perhaps because of them, Lyn was angry. "I get better marks at school than he does!" she exclaimed.

But the Captain had left.

When the Prince spoke to the dragons the next morning, most said they did not want to leave. "We are content here and can do as we please, so why leave?" Some wavered but decided the journey would cause them too many hardships. In the end, only a few chose to go. There was an elderly couple with their baby great-granddaughter, a pretty little thing of two passings. "Take her at least," they pleaded. "We long to go with you, but we are old and though we still fly well, we would slow you down."

Neither the Prince nor the Captain would hear of their staying behind. "If you can get over the pass, come. We will not be flying long distances each day."

Another couple with two children asked to go, and, to Lyn's surprise, two young dragons and the flirtatious dragoness of the evening before. She told the Prince what had happened. "I think she is going because she wants to make an impression on Dathir."

"I don't think much of those two dragons' motives, either," said Greg. "I was speaking with them and suspect they are going because they are taken with our warriors' prowess."

"That may be so, yet a poor motive may turn into a good decision. The hardships of this journey will soon prove them," was the Captain's brief comment.

Just before they left, the Prince told the new members of his band that he was now putting himself under the Captain's command for the whole of the journey and the others were to do the same.

"Take over," he said to the Captain, who at once told them in what order they were to fly and then gave the command to leave. With cries of farewell they were off. The Chief and his companions, now free, yelled curses and insults after them but made no attempt to follow.

To their great delight, the children were on Lorimon again. "How long do you think this return trip will take us?" Greg asked him.

"Much longer than it took us to get here. The babies are no problem and we will all take turns carrying the two young children. The three elderly dragons, Alamirna's brother, and the other young one and his sister will set our pace."

Nevertheless they made reasonably good time to the pass and when they reached it the weather was perfect. Even the elderly dragons made their way through it without too much difficulty except for considerable panting. Everyone was greatly relieved and there was much rejoicing when they halted a good way down the long L-shaped valley.

The northern dragons, though unused to flying in an orderly formation, kept pretty well to the places the Captain had assigned them, except for the flirtatious dragoness and one of the young dragons. Whenever the Captain was flying ahead of them, they would slip out of their places to another part of the line. When ordered back, they would complain that they did not see why they could not fly beside anyone they wanted to. Each time they dropped down to rest, the dragoness would manage to land beside Dathir and when he asked her please not to trouble him, she sulked.

By the third evening she had had enough. She talked with the two young dragons until they were as discontented as she.

The next morning she and one of the dragons said they were leaving and going back. "Your place sounds horribly dull, nothing but laws. We are going back where we are free to do anything we want to."

The two of them urged the other dragon to return with them and he, after some hesitation, did so.

"I think he would have remained if they had not talked him into going back," Lyn commented to Lorimon as she watched them fly off.

"He did not have to listen to them. He did, and he has made his choice."

Despite their best efforts the older and younger dragons did slow everyone down. The Captain decided to divide the group; the larger part went on ahead. They did the searching for a good site to camp, the hunting, and preparing dinner. When the second half, consisting of the older and younger members accompanied by a few warriors, arrived, everything was ready. In this way much time was saved.

On the fifth night when they were enjoying their evening meal, one of the dragons on watch called out that a dragon was approaching. The Captain and several warriors at once leapt up and then in a few moments dropped down again. With them was the young dragon who had been persuaded to leave two days earlier. He begged to be allowed to rejoin them.

The Prince asked why he had come back.

"When I first asked to come with you it was only because I thought it would be a great thing to be a warrior. I did not pay much attention to everything else you said. After a couple of days of actually being with you, when I saw how disciplined the warriors were, I began to wonder if I really wanted that life. The other two pointed out how hard it would be; that, if not actually lying, you were probably exaggerating greatly as to how wonderful your land was. I knew perfectly well that you were not lying and never would, but it was a good excuse to go back and so I did. As we flew, something kept nagging inside me. I tried hard not to listen to it and succeeded until we came to the pass. As we came through to our side, I suddenly could pretend no longer and knew that I would regret forever not having followed you and your ways, hard though they might be. So I turned back, despite the others' jeers. They also said you would look on me as a failure and refuse to have anything to do with me. This time I did not listen. I have flown back as fast as I could, and beg you to give me another chance."

"It is a braver thing to admit one has been wrong than to win a combat, and we are glad to have you with us again," said the Prince. "Now eat with us, for you look tired and hungry."

"I have only eaten once since leaving you,

because I was afraid of losing your track," said the young dragon, adding many grateful thanks and promising to be as helpful as he could – a promise which he faithfully kept.

Each evening when the dragons were lying around resting and chatting, Lyn and Greg enjoyed playing with the lively little baby dragoness and so the Prince put them in charge of her. "Her great-grandparents," he said, "fly bravely but are really too tired at the end of each day's flight to take care of such an active little one."

So they watched over her at every stop. She was tied up in a warm package like the other baby and each time Greg first had to untie the knots. Then they fed her and played with her and afterward she was tied up again and a dragon carried her. At night she slept tucked warmly between them and appeared to be enjoying her strange nursemaids.

"We don't have to worry about stretching our legs now," said Lyn, as she chased the baby who was scuttling after a mouse. "She stretches them for us."

One day, the flying was bad. In the morning there was fog, then a couple of showers, and the Captain ordered them down early.

Most of the dragons happened to be in the air for one reason or another when a dragon cried out, "Danger! Danger! Take to the air!"

Those on the ground flung themselves upwards at once, and Lyn and Greg who had taken the baby down to a stream for a drink suddenly found themselves alone on the ground, which was trembling beneath them.

"An earthquake!" exclaimed Greg.

Lyn looked around and gave a cry of alarm. "Look!" she yelled. From either side of a group of trees a short distance away was pouring a huge herd of large-horned cattle. They were right in the path of that mad stampede.

"Up that tree!" yelled Greg. "I'll hand the baby to you!"

Lyn raced to the tree and swung herself up onto a branch, then turned to reach down for the dragoness. To her horror, she saw that Greg would not make it. The baby had chosen this moment to squirm wildly and almost threw herself out of his arms. He tripped over her flailing tail and nearly fell. Just before the thundering herd was upon him, he managed to reach the shelter of two trees whose trunks almost touched each other. He crouched between them while the now terrified child wailed and struggled desperately to get out of his arms.

Lyn clung to the tree, sick with fear for her brother, and pressed her face against a branch so as not to see him being trampled. She kept it there until she heard Lorimon calling her. She looked up. There was Lorimon, Dathir, and Greg as white-faced as herself but safe and uninjured. She practically fell out of the tree and ran over and hugged him, crying with relief.

Greg hugged her back. "The herd divided and rushed past on each side of the trees. They were so close that one brushed me! The real problem was the baby, whom I could barely hold. In fact, as the last few went by, she finally jerked herself out of my arms and fell right in front of one of them! Luckily it just snorted and shied away at the sight of her!"

"Where is she?"

Greg did not have to answer. The baby had begun to wail and a dragoness was trying to comfort her.

Everyone praised Greg's bravery and presence of mind.

"I cannot wait to tell my father," the Prince said with a chuckle. "You did not know it, but he was very reluctant to permit you and your sister to accompany Lorimon and Dathir on this expedition. He felt responsible for you and your safety. Now I can tell him that had it not been for you, that little one would surely have been killed."

"If you were back home, you would probably receive a medal or reward," said Lyn, who was just beginning to recover from her fright. She said this as a joke, but the word "reward" brought back her dreams of somehow finding a treasure or earning a reward that would make them rich. Now Greg had done something very brave and there was no hope of a reward. Or was there? What about the King's and Queen's gorgeous jeweled collars which she and Greg had once saved from the Dark Dragons? Might there not be a few loose gems somewhere? If so, the King might give them at least one, since the dragons did not know their value. When they were back at the palace she would watch for a chance to speak to the Queen and say she wanted one for her mother, which would be true.

Until then she decided not to say anything to Greg because she knew he was annoyed with her. During the trip she had been worrying a good deal because his admiration for Dathir was growing, and she suspected that this was not good for either of them. All the warriors did aerial acrobatics to keep limber for combat. This was normal. Dathir's, however, were growing more and more spectacular, and one day she heard Greg egging him on to show the northern dragons what excellent fliers their southern counterparts were.

Next he went up with Dathir and clung tightly to the pad while Dathir did some very mild maneuvers. This gave Greg the sensation of being a daredevil, and when Lyn begged him not to, he pooh-poohed her fears for his safety. In desperation she went to the Captain, who promptly put an end to Greg's and Dathir's acrobatics. Dathir did not mind, but Greg was put out with Lyn for stopping his fun; and so Lyn did not tell him of her plan of asking the Queen for a loose jewel, if there were any.

The remainder of the flight was uneventful. When they were still a couple days away from the border, the Captain sent a warrior ahead to warn the King of the arrival of these newcomers, and to bring back carrying nets in which the older and younger dragons could be carried when they were tired. This would enable the group to make a longer day's journey since they would not have to stop as frequently. The warriors, being anxious to get back, were greatly relieved. "We have never been away so long from our families and they must be terribly worried about us," one of them told Lyn.

The Captain was equally relieved, but for a different reason. "We left secretly in order that the Dark Dragons might not know there were fewer warriors guarding the border. Sooner or later they are bound to guess and may attack."

Lyn had grown to like the Captain. He could be very stern with those who disobeyed his orders, but he was kindness itself to the weary and discouraged and especially to the timid little dragoness over whom he watched with fatherly care.

"What will happen to her and her brother?" Lyn asked the Prince.

"The Captain is going to take them into his own family. He has been a good father to his children and will be so to them, and his motherly wife is just what those poor, maltreated children need."

At long last, late one afternoon they came over the final pass and landed at one of the northern stations of the Green Dragon kingdom. Several dragons flew out to greet them, and the newcomers were overwhelmed at the friendliness of their welcome, the sight of the solid houses, and all the signs of contentment and prosperity.

"Do all the dragons live in such fine houses?" Alamirna asked Lyn. She noticed that Alamirna had grown very silent, and thought it was from astonishment.

"Wait until you see the palace," she told her.

"That is where Lorimon dwells, is it not?" Alamirna asked sadly.

"Only when he is not at his station."

The next day the Prince led them to the palace where the King and Queen, wearing the beautiful jeweled collars (their second best) were waiting on the terrace to greet them. With them was the Master, the Prince of the Dragon-Cousins and his wife, and of course, the Princess. In a semi-circle around the lawn were several dozen other dragons and Dragon-Cousins who had come to participate in the unheard-of event. At the back of the terrace, tucked safely against the wall of the palace, was Alan. A Dragon-Cousin was beside him and was telling him what was happening. Greg waved. The Dragon-Cousin saw it and spoke quickly to Alan, who waved back.

The sight of the palace and the royal family overwhelmed the northern dragons. At first they uttered exclamations of astonishment and then fell silent and landed quietly.

"I cannot believe that we were actually *invited* to come here!" Greg heard one of the dragons exclaim.

"To think that I felt so badly at leaving my cave and even wondered if I would ever find anything as comfortable," said the young mother.

"Do you think they will share some of their things with us?" whispered another.

Radkar heard that one. "They are not the kind who do not share," he said in his usual gruff manner.

The Prince introduced the newcomers and made a speech about their journey, but he never finished it. His little son was present, held firmly in his mother's arms. She was so intent on listening to her husband, however, that she inadvertently relaxed her hold. He at once shot forward to his father, squealing with delight. Everyone laughed and the tension of the meeting was broken. The King and Queen greeted their new subjects and paid particular attention to the children.

Then the Captain called for quiet and the King, looking very regal, addressed the assembly. His manner was kind, but his words were uncompromising.

"My Queen and I welcome you in the name of the Great One, you, who like us, are descendants of the Green Dragons who once dwelt near the smoking mountain. Before you chose to come, you were told about our ways and the manner in which we live. If you are willing to obey the laws of the Great One and of this realm, you are most welcome.

"First you must dwell for a while on the Mount and be taught by the Master of Wisdom, as have all of us. Later, if you still wish to remain with us, I will find homes for all of you. Still later, when the Master in his wisdom knows each of you is ready in mind and heart, you will be given the gold armband to wear as we do in pride and gratitude. Then you will indeed no longer be strangers or visitors, but our own."

For a few moments the northern dragons did not speak; most of them were weeping. At last Alamirna's grandfather spoke for them all and thanked the King, ending simply with, "I know there is no way we can ever express our gratitude to you or to your son and the warriors who brought us safely here at great peril to themselves, except by being faithful. That, I promise you, we will all strive to be." And all the dragons around him added their promises.

Refreshments were brought. The dragons were totally unprepared for the manner in which they were served and stared in astonishment at the Dragon-Cousins who passed among them with plates and bowls on their backs. They hesitated. The Princess, who guessed their embarrassment, quickly came forward and took one of the bowls and handed it to Alamirna's grandfather, and then a plate to another dragon. Soon all were enjoying themselves.

Lyn and Greg made their way over to Alan and sat down beside him. He was delighted to have them back.

"I'm dying to hear about your explorations! You don't know how worried we have been because you were away so long! Then word came that you were safe and were bringing back more dragons. Everyone was so excited! The King sent for me so I would be here to greet you. I'm going to stay with you here for a while, because the Mount will be crowded and the Master is afraid I might get hurt.

"Tell me all about it while we eat. I knew there were going to be refreshments and asked the Queen if we could have them together."

The Dragon-Cousin who had disappeared now returned with plates and bowls and they settled down to a long, exciting talk.

Just before the dragons were escorted to the Mount, the King made another announcement. "I, and all present, thank our brave warriors who, led by the Captain, so courageously made this extraordinary flight which will be told of forever in our tales. Their families have been most anxious over their long absence, and so I grant each one ten days leave."

The warriors flapped their wings enthusiastically and gave a rousing cheer.

Dathir laughed. "What about Lorimon and me, my uncle? We not only have had our leave, but have long overstayed it."

The King chuckled. "You two have certainly overstayed your leave as I have never known any other dragon to do! Your penalty will be to come to dinner and tell us all about your travels and discoveries."

CHAPTER 7
The King's Judgment

A most pleasant time followed. Everyone wanted to hear the story of the expedition. Lorimon, Dathir, Lyn and Greg were praised over and over again. This did not seem to affect Lorimon, but "Dathir is getting more and more pleased with himself," he confided anxiously to Lyn one day, "and I am very worried about him."

"The same is happening to Greg, and I am worried about him, too," said Lyn with a troubled expression.

It was true. Greg heard himself praised so many times for his rescue of the baby dragoness that he thought of himself as quite a hero.

"He really isn't like this usually," Lyn went on, "so I hope it's only temporary. At least he can't get into trouble here, and once we're back home, he certainly can't go around bragging that he saved a baby dragoness!"

She laughed at the idea, and then said wickedly, "How is Alamirna today?"

Since their return, Lorimon had been going at least twice a day to the Mount. "Just to see how the newcomers are doing," he explained; but it was noticeable that after a few general inquiries he spent most of his time with Alamirna.

He chuckled, then said proudly, "She is a lovely dragoness. Even the Master is surprised at her great desire to learn our laws and her quick understanding of his teachings."

Lyn giggled. "Then don't you think you should propose to her soon or else some other dragon will get her?"

Lorimon shook his head. "If she cares for me, and I think she does, she will not accept another suitor. But should she prefer another to me . . . well then, I shall try to be content in seeing her happy."

"I was only teasing, but *do* go and ask her. It will save her a good deal of wondering what she is going to do in this new place." What Lyn did not say was that Alamirna had confided to her that she was feeling more and more like a rough, untaught stranger who had nothing compared with . . . say, Lorimon, who was the nephew of the King and lived in such a beautiful palace.

"You are *not* rough and untaught, and what you don't have doesn't matter here. How could you think such a thing of Lorimon?" Lyn had said reproachfully to her, but Alamirna had remained unconvinced.

So Lyn urged Lorimon to ask her. "You are not going to change your mind, are you? So why wait to offer her happiness?"

"You are right," Lorimon replied. "I shall go right now."

All the royal family and the three children were on the lawn when Lorimon returned. "She refused me," he said disconsolately. "And yet I think she cares for me."

"I know she does!" exclaimed Lyn. "But she is overwhelmed by the fact that she is a stranger who, only because of the King's kindness, is allowed to live here, while you are the King's nephew."

"I shall go and talk with her," said the Princess getting up and spreading her wings. "I know just how she feels. *Overwhelmed* is the right word. I felt the same way when the Prince asked me to marry him."

After a while she returned. "If I were you, Lorimon," she said as she settled herself beside the Prince, "I would go back and ask her again."

Lorimon was off in a flash and came back much later carrying a beautiful jug. Everyone laughed and, before he said a word, congratulated him on his betrothal to Alamirna.

Greg was dumbfounded. "How do you know?" he demanded.

The Princess answered. "Perhaps you do not know our custom. When a dragoness accepts his proposal, the dragon brings her a bowl or jug or plate, then at their first meal after their wedding the dragoness serves him something in it."

"That is a beautiful custom," said Lyn. "If you are taking it to Alamirna now, why don't you fill it with flowers the way we do in our world?"

"Flowers? Why?" queried Lorimon, looking puzzled.

"Look, I'll show you what I mean." Lyn ran over to the lawn by the farthest corner of the terrace where a few bright red and yellow flowers had escaped being crushed by the dragons. She picked a bunch, then took the jug from Lorimon and filled it as attractively as she could.

"That's very pretty, Lyn," said Greg approvingly. "You have a real talent for that sort of thing."

Lyn gave the jug back to Lorimon saying, "Carry it upright so the flowers don't fall out, and tell Alamirna to put water in it."

"Why?" asked Lorimon again, looking more puzzled than ever.

"To keep them alive, of course."

Lorimon suddenly remembered his manners, thanked her politely, and flew off carefully, holding the jug upright.

"What a strange custom," murmured the Queen, "but then, my dears, some of our customs must seem strange to you."

Later on, Dathir felt he ought to go to the Mount and tell Alamirna how pleased he was that she had accepted his brother. Lyn, Greg, and Alan went along to add their congratulations. Lorimon had left and they found Alamirna admiring the jug from every possible angle. There were no flowers in it. Before they left, Greg, who had been wandering around, called Lyn over. Behind a tree on the edge of the plateau were the flowers.

They doubled up with laughter. "I remember now," said Lyn when she could stop laughing, "I once described our window boxes to Lorimon and he could not understand why we tried to make flowers grow where they did not grow naturally."

"No wonder the Queen thought we had strange

customs," Greg replied. "Come on, I think Dathir wants to leave." They ran back, still laughing.

Lyn managed to have her private talk with the Queen about the jewels. The Queen told her that there were no loose jewels because the Dragon-Cousins, in their gratitude for the dragons' constant and loyal protection, had used up every single jewel in making the dragons' collars and bracelets for the Queen. To her own surprise, Lyn was relieved rather than disappointed. She had a haunting feeling that taking an extraordinary jewel back from this world to hers would cause nothing but trouble.

The day after Lorimon's betrothal was one Greg would never forget to the end of his life. The King, who was usually taciturn, had been quite talkative and had entertained them with tales of his youth. "The Dark King of those days was young and warlike and our warriors had to be very alert. We never knew when the next attack was going to take place." He ended his tales with, "Now there has been peace along the border for many passings, which is good for the kingdom, although the young warriors find it boring.

"Which reminds me. I have heard that some of the young warriors, especially along the northern part of the border, are daring each other to fly farther and farther over the Dark Dragons' realm. They know perfectly well it is foolhardy and that they lay themselves open to severe penalties, but since there is no definite command against it, they do it. Tomorrow I must speak to the Captain and we will decide what is to be done."

He went on to speak of other matters. Lyn noticed Greg scowling at the King's words.

"Why did you scowl like that?" she asked him when they were alone. "What difference does the King's order make to you?"

"Dathir told me about those flights and I am going with him once, for the excitement of it."

"But it's dangerous!"

"No, it isn't. The warriors do it all the time. The King is probably overcautious. A King has to be, of course."

"You heard what he said."

"He only said casually, 'I must speak to the Captain,' and he will probably forget all about it. Anyway, tomorrow is not today. Dathir said he would take me today. I asked him yesterday."

"But Lorimon is going to take us to a dragon dancing class and then we are going to visit the baby dragoness, and see if she remembers us."

"You go. I don't care about the dancing class. It's bad enough to have to go to them at home! Here's Dathir. Dathir, I'm ready. I didn't ask Lyn to come; she'd be afraid."

"No, she is very brave. I have seen her in danger," Dathir replied seriously.

"I know she is," Greg admitted belatedly. "Anyway, she is going off this afternoon with Lorimon."

Lyn was hurt and furious. "All right, go ahead and disobey the King and get yourself into trouble for all I care," she said, and walked off in a huff. They rarely quarreled, and Greg knew he was in the wrong this time.

"I'll make it up with her tonight," he thought to himself.

"What is this about disobeying the King?" Dathir demanded. "The King must be obeyed. Has he given orders not to fly over the border?"

"No," said Greg hurriedly. This was true, but he knew perfectly well what was in the King's mind. "After all, didn't you say that most of the young warriors do it?"

"Yes . . . there is no definite command against it."

"As I told you, there is still no definite command against it. But, if you are afraid, then leave me here and go back to your northern post until you are old enough to be on the border!"

He knew that would irritate Dathir. It did. "Very well, let us be off." Dathir was breathing smoke.

To do Greg justice, he never for a moment thought there was any danger in this escapade. He knew the Dark Dragons rarely went into the northern mountains because they preferred the warm plains. He also knew Dathir did it just so as to be able to say that he had ventured into the Dark Dragons' territory, and Greg wanted the fun of being able to boast that he, too, had been there.

As they neared the border, Dathir caught sight of a friend and called out, "Come on, Garan! Fly with me over the border!"

Garan joined them and they crossed over the border, keeping low between the trees so as not to be seen by the border patrol. When they were in the

Dark Dragons' land, they flew a little higher, but still only just over the treetops. Sometimes they were so low that branches brushed Greg's legs, and once when Dathir ducked between two treetops, a branch springing back nearly swept Greg off.

"Look out!" he yelled. "I nearly lost my grip!"

"Be quiet!" Dathir said urgently. "We are turning back now. I should never have brought you!" He did a slow, sweeping turn, still just brushing the treetops.

They were nearly at the border when Garan gave a warning cry: two Dark Dragons had leapt up from a nearby hiding place. One attacked Garan and the other went for Dathir who, hampered by Greg, could only duck aside. His attacker missed his blow, but a blast of flame hit Greg's arm, and he gave a cry of pain.

Dathir folded his wings and dropped fast, saying as he did, "Fall off and hide as soon as I touch the ground!"

But there was no need for that order. He came down so hard that Greg was thrown off, and luckily for him, landed in a shrub. Breathless, he picked himself up. A terrific combat was going on overhead but there was so much smoke and flame he could not see what was happening. For a moment he was too shaken to hide, then he ducked under a tree and looked up again. A Green Dragon was being driven down by his opponent who was fiercely harrying him. For a moment his heart stopped; then he turned to run just as two more Green Dragons swept into view and joined in the fight. The wounded dragon fell to the ground where he lay bleeding terribly and feebly moving his wings. For a horrible moment Greg thought it was Dathir, then realized it was Garan. Dathir landed a moment later with one of the other Green Dragons, and the two of them at once began stanching Garan's wounds. Dathir was weeping as he did so.

After a while, two more dragons arrived with a carrying net, along with leaves and ointments which they carefully placed on Garan's wounds. Then they gently placed the net under him and flew off with him. Dathir did not realize that Greg had been hurt. He was one of the dragons carrying the net and he called to Greg over his shoulder that the other dragon would carry him back to the palace. Greg stumbled toward the remaining dragon, holding his arm.

"You are hurt," said the dragon. "On my back quickly, and hold these leaves over your burn."

Instead of taking him to the palace, he first took Greg to the nearest border station where his wound was bound up, and then flew with him to the Mount where he would be better cared for. It was a long flight and by the time they arrived, Greg was dizzy and worn out with pain, but most of all with the misery of knowing that he had been responsible for the tragedy.

He anxiously asked the Healer who was tending to his burn if Garan's wounds were serious. "Yes, very serious. The Master is with him now. We do not know if he is going to live."

"It was my fault," Greg sobbed. "I knew we

shouldn't go there."

The Dragon-Cousin looked at him gravely. "You all knew you should not cross the border. Now you have all paid for it."

Nevertheless he was very kind and made Greg lie down. Then he brought him a drink that soothed the pain and let him doze off. When he woke again he was greatly comforted by finding Lyn and Alan beside him.

Lyn had had a very different sort of outing. First, Lorimon had taken her to a dancing class as he had promised he would. The dancing master was elderly and somewhat plump but, Lorimon said, "The best dancing teacher in the kingdom." When they arrived, a group of young dragonesses were just finishing a graceful dance known as the "Dragonesses' Spring Dance". A dozen young dragons were about to begin the "Warriors' Dance."

"Remember," said the teacher, "curl your tails up, beat your wings in unison and when I call, blow flame first to the right and then to the left. Now up you go."

This dance is done in pairs, and so the youngsters faced each other in six couples a little distance above the ground while the teacher called instructions up to them. "Keep a straight line. Last couple, you are too far from the others. Now beat your wings in unison. Good. Now, heads right – flame. Heads left – flame," and the dancers blew flame vigorously to the right and left.

After that dance the youngsters crowded excitedly around Lyn, fascinated by this strange person.

"Do you dance in your world?" asked one of the dragonesses.

"Of course we do," Lyn incautiously replied.

"Do show us one of your dances, please," they begged.

Lyn was non-plussed. She loved to dance, especially Scottish reels, but her dances needed music. At last she decided on the Highland Fling and the Sword Dance. The latter one intrigued the young onlookers. She had used sticks for swords and two of the dragons quickly drew a large X on each side of her.

"Now show us again and we will follow you," they said.

She did the steps slowly and the youngsters tried to imitate her, bouncing up and down energetically and flapping their wings. "I understand now," one called to the other over Lyn's head. "The point is to see who can get through the steps the fastest." And they bounced more energetically than ever.

Lyn laughed so hard she had to stop dancing. When the dragons asked what the rules were, she made some up on the spot. "Only one beat of wings for each step. You must not touch the lines. You must follow the pattern exactly. Jump straight across, then to the right, then to the left, then all the way around, stopping in each quarter."

She left them bouncing happily and she and Lorimon went on to visit the baby dragoness. Her great-grandparents were still very weary from the journey and she was being cared for by another couple. To Lyn's great pleasure, the little one remembered her and scurried over, squealing with delight. Lyn would have gladly played with her for hours, but like all the very young, in the middle of a game she curled up and went to sleep.

Back at the palace, the King told her briefly what had happened to Greg and Dathir. A few moments later, Lyn was again on Lorimon, Alan with her, and they were heading towards the Mount, bringing with them orders from the King for both Dathir and Greg to appear before him for judgment.

The curative powers of the ointments and leaves used on his burns were so excellent that by the next morning the pain had greatly subsided, and the Master said he could be taken to the King. Alan and Lyn went with him.

"What do you think will happen?" Lyn asked anxiously while in flight.

"I don't know. I suppose he will send me back through the Door," Greg said as calmly as he could. He was very grateful to Lyn for not saying, "I told you so," as she occasionally did, and did not want to make her unhappy by letting her see how miserable he felt. He tried to sound optimistic. "After all, can you imagine the King hurting me in any way?" After a moment he added in a low tone, "It's what penalty Dathir will get that worries me. I may be sent back through the Door, but he has to stay here, and it's all my fault."

Dathir, along with the Captain of the Border Guard, was already there when they arrived, as were Lorimon and the Prince. Dathir made no excuses. When asked, he said frankly that he had done wrong and blamed himself for Garan's injuries and for having endangered Greg's life. He did not say a word about Greg having egged him on.

"Now you, Child from another world, what have you to say for yourself?" the King asked Greg in a stern voice. Greg had no intention of lying, but as he later said, even if he had tried to, he could not have lied with the King's eyes fixed upon him. There is a special power in the eyes of the King of the Green Dragons when he wishes to use it, a power which commands the truth. No one can look him in the face and lie.

Lyn, who had placed herself beside her brother, determined to give him what support she could, felt the power though it was not directed towards her. Afterwards Greg always said that powerful though the King's glance was, yet it was a good power and gave him the extra strength he needed to take as much of the blame as possible on himself. Lyn sensed that this pleased the King. Nevertheless, his voice was severe when he passed the sentences.

"You, Child from Earth, must return to your own world. You may stay on the Mount without leaving it until your burn is healed, as I would not have you leave us while injured. Lyn and Alan may remain in our realm and move about freely until such time as they, too, must return to their own place."

To Dathir he spoke in an even sterner voice. "You, Dathir, a member of the Border Guard, have disgraced yourself. Therefore you may no longer be a warrior. Instead, I assign you to the messenger service of this land. However, since you are but a young warrior, this penalty will only last until you have proved to me that you have become more responsible. Then you may return to the Border Guard." The King's voice softened a little. "Dathir, my nephew, I urge you to first go to the Master and speak long with him before you take up your new post. It is he who can best teach you how to shorten the time of your penalty and . . . ," the King made a long pause, "how to accept it."

A tremor had passed through Dathir when he heard the sentence. Lyn could not bear his anguished expression, but all he did was to bow his head in acknowledgment and then fly off without a backward glance. Lorimon went with him.

The children were taken back to the Mount. No one felt like speaking – Greg, because he felt miserable and his arm was aching, and Lyn, because she did not know what to do. She did not want to leave, and yet she knew she would feel terrible and uncomfortable if she remained, enjoying herself, while Greg was sent ignominiously home. Alan kept quiet because it wasn't his trouble and he didn't want to barge in.

With one accord, they went straight to the Master and told him what had happened. "Since it's my fault, I'm the only one who should go home. That's only fair, isn't it?" Greg insisted.

"Do you think the King was only being kind, but would really like all of us to leave?" Lyn asked.

Alan still kept silent.

"You do not speak?" the Master said to him.

"I think the King meant just what he said. He gave the penalties and the matter is finished. I can't imagine him holding anything against anybody, even Greg and Dathir. Greg, I am terribly sorry for you, but I've been thinking it over and I don't know if Lyn and I should go. You heard what the King said about our going when we *must* go."

"You are learning well," said the Master.

"Master, it is you who have taught me."

Suddenly, Lyn realized that while they had been exploring, Alan had been learning from the Master, and she envied him. When they returned to their own world, she promised herself, she would ask him to tell her what he had learned.

The next few days were miserable for the twins. Greg tried to be cheerful for Lyn's sake, but as the passing of each day shortened his stay, it grew harder and harder. What made it worse, of course, was the realization that it was all his own fault. He was partly consoled by the knowledge that Garan would recover eventually.

Lyn knew perfectly well he was covering up his misery for her sake, and that cost her many a private tear. How could she continue to enjoy being here, knowing he was sitting unhappy and alone on the beach of Smugglers' Cove? Yet, what troubled her the most was that Dathir never came to speak to the Master. She longed to ask Lorimon what his brother was doing, but Lorimon had gone for a few days to his station in the south.

CHAPTER 8
Lorimon and Dathir

Under the Healer's able ministrations, Greg's burn healed rapidly and when the bandage of leaves was removed, the Master said there would probably be no scar. "Tomorrow you must return to the King and he will take you to the Door."

Lyn, Greg and Alan were spending a last, sad afternoon together when Lorimon flew in. He was very upset and called out as soon as he saw them, "Has Dathir been here?"

They ran over. "No, we have been wondering where he was. We haven't seen him since the day we were before the King," said Greg.

Lorimon asked the Master and all the dragons who happened to be on the Mount. No one had seen him.

"He has not been seen since that day. I thought, of course, he would come to you, Master, after he had had time to think things over a bit, and so I thought it best to leave him alone for a while. I was heartsick about him and worried, but was confident that if he listened to you, he would be able to face himself and his disgrace.

"A short time ago a friend asked me if Dathir had been transferred to a southern station. Without showing any alarm, I asked why he thought so, and was told that the day after our uncle passed sentence on him, he was seen flying over the southernmost part of the realm. Now I fear terribly for him."

With a quick farewell to the Master, Lorimon was off with a great rush of wings, and he did not return until just before sunrise the next morning.

"I have searched everywhere," he said wearily to the Master. "To the North and the South I have flown and asked all of his friends, waking up some of them to do so, which they did not appreciate. No one has seen him except two Dragon-Cousins who, on what was the day after his sentence, saw a dragon with markings like Dathir's flying across the southwest boundaries of their land."

"But where could he go?" Lyn asked in astonishment. "I thought you told us there is a huge desert there."

"There is. But remember? The evening after we discovered 'Smoketop' and were so excited, he said to me, 'There is still the south to be explored; on our next long leave we must see if we can cross the desert.' He is so ashamed, that I am afraid he has fled there."

"Fled?" Lyn remembered sadly the King's words about Dathir. "You mean he couldn't face failure . . . poor Dathir! What are you going to do?"

"I am going to ask my uncle's permission to go after him. I know he is miserably unhappy and will soon realize not only how wrong he was to flee, but also that he cannot flee from himself. Then he may need me to help him return; his pride and self-confidence have been so shattered. If only I *can* help him," he ended sadly in a low, anguished voice.

Greg jumped up. "Let me come with you! I am the one who urged him on. Perhaps he will listen to me."

"The King said you must return to your own world."

"I am going to ask him to let me go with you."

"Master . . . ," Lorimon began.

"Go," said the Master, "and go swiftly, or it may be too late for Dathir."

Alan remained on the Mount, saying, "I couldn't help you, and since the new dragons have all been given homes, I can stay here again with the Master."

Lyn refused to be left behind and Lorimon took them to the King. He urgently begged the King for leave to search for his brother.

The King was reluctant to give his consent. "I fear losing you also, Lorimon. You who have been a second son to me."

In the end, though, he did give permission. "Go swiftly then, Lorimon, since the Master said to, and take whatever you may need."

He was even more reluctant to let Greg go, but Greg pleaded earnestly, "It was my fault. Dathir was going to ask you until I practically accused him of lacking the courage to fly into the Dark Dragons' land."

"You were both to blame," said the King quietly. "Dathir by far the most, as he is full grown and has been a warrior for four passings."

After much thought, the King leaned over and touched him gently and said, "You may go, and when you return, if you do, your sentence will be lifted."

Lorimon was impatient to leave. "We must start at once. I did not need the Master's words, for my heart urges me to hurry."

"I am going, too," said Lyn.

"No, indeed! You had nothing to do with this. Who knows what we might meet? There may be danger," Greg said. He did not mean to sound patronizing, but Lyn thought he did.

"Of course I am going, so don't put on airs," she snapped back at him, then remembered where she was and turned red. "I beg your pardon," she apologized to the King and Lorimon. "We really get on very well together. It is just . . . um . . . just . . ."

"That you are brother and sister," said the King with a slight chuckle. "I have a younger sister, and she still scolds me at times, though she loves me dearly. Yes, you may go with Lorimon and your brother. Perhaps in the end they will both be glad that I sent you with them."

With the help of two Dragon-Cousins, all was made ready very quickly. Lorimon had two carrying baskets; one held provisions and the other gourds of water.

"I am worried about flying over the desert," said Lorimon. "As I do not know how wide it is nor have I heard of anyone who has ever flown more than half a day's journey across it, we must take plenty of water."

While the baskets were being prepared, the children hurriedly ate breakfast and Greg sharpened his beloved knife. Then they were in the air and flying south as fast as Lorimon dared go with them on his back. They flew steadily and he did not drop down until he was at the southernmost boundary of the Dragon-Cousins' principality. Here there were only a few, small, scattered villages and he stopped at each one to ask if anyone had seen a dragon flying southward a few days previously.

In two of the villages several Dragon-Cousins had seen a dragon and could describe him.

"That was Dathir," said Lorimon. "Did any of you watch him until he was out of sight and see which way he was going?"

"Well, I did not watch until he was actually out of sight, but from what I saw he seemed to be heading towards the desert, which I thought unusual," answered one of them. "Sometimes, though, a warrior is sent to check the border, so I supposed that was what he was doing. Anything wrong?"

"I am afraid so." The Dragon-Cousin politely asked no further questions. While Lorimon took a short rest, their friendly hosts brought them food and drink. Then on they went. The rolling green hills below them flattened out and the rich, flower-studded fields turned into an unbroken sea of tall, green grasses.

Lyn, who was in front, lay flat along Lorimon's neck and watched the grasses sway and dip in a long, rolling motion as the wind swept over them. Every now and then a stronger gust would bow their tops so low that she glimpsed a patch of bare earth or brown rock that appeared for an instant like a lost island, and then vanished again as the grass lifted up. Once in a small, open place she saw a rabbit family: mother, father, and four half-grown young ones sitting up with their ears pricked and alert, who cowered and then vanished when Lorimon's shadow passed over them. In another spot the grasses parted to show a fox carrying a fat rat back to its family.

She was so absorbed in watching the grass that she was startled by Greg's exclamation, "Look at the desert!" She sat up quickly. Still a good distance away, the gray-green sea of grass ended abruptly, cut off by a vast expanse of yellow-brown sand. It went on and on, flat and bleak without the slightest sign of any vegetation. "Grim and foreboding," were the words that came to her mind, but she kept them to herself. Greg, as usual, came right out with how he felt.

"It looks as though it were waiting to swallow up anyone who dares cross it. At least on foot," he added belatedly.

"Yes, we have Lorimon's wings," said Lyn as optimistically as she could manage. She hoped her voice did not sound as shaky as she feared it did. Greg was right; it did look ready to swallow up anyone who tried to conquer it. *Grim* and *foreboding* were too weak a description, she decided. *Ominous* was more like it.

Before they were really close, Lorimon circled and landed where his sharp eyes had seen a Dragon-Cousin watching them. This Dragon-Cousin, Wollimar by name, was less talkative than most of his kind, but he was friendly. He occasionally hunted in this area, he told them, because of the different sorts of game that could be found here, especially a fat sand snake that was difficult to catch because it looked so much like the grasses.

Yes, he had seen a dragon some days back. He was flying low and so his markings could be plainly seen. He was certain the dragon had seen him, even though he had not given the customary dip of his head in answer to the Dragon-Cousin's greeting. From his description there could be no doubt. It was Dathir. He had not returned.

Leaving the twins on the ground, Lorimon, flying very high, went out over the desert. When he came back he reported that there was nothing but desert in the direction Dathir had taken. "He certainly would not have gone towards the land on the right, as that is the edge of the Dark Dragon territory. Nor to the left towards the sea, as the coastland is much like our own land, and many have flown far along it. No, he must have headed straight across. Many of us, myself among them, have flown a little way into the desert just to see what it was like. But, as I told you, none have ever glimpsed the other side. Yet, it must end somewhere."

"How far do you plan to go?" Greg asked.

"As far as a supply of water can take me and bring me back. We dragons can go without food for a long time, but water we need."

"We do also," Lyn said.

"I shall rest until very early morning and start

while the air above the sands is still cool, and fly as far as I can; then rest, and fly again. If when half my water is gone there is still no end of the desert, I shall turn back.

"Now that I have had more time to think about this flight over the desert, I think it would be wiser for you two to remain here with Wollimar. If I do not return, he can guide you back to his land. Since we go there all the time, a dragon will take you back to the palace."

"We want to go with you, and the King said we could!" expostulated Greg.

Lyn glanced up at Lorimon. He looked so sorrowful and lonely that she threw her arms around his neck. "I know we may slow you down a little, but we love Dathir, too. Besides," she sobbed, "I can't bear to think of your going alone. I'm sure there is some way we can be of help."

"It would be a great comfort to have you with me," Lorimon said gently. "I spoke only out of concern for your safety. Very well: we faced the mountains together, now let us face the desert."

Wollimar had been listening intently. "Before you start across that desert, you need a good rest and plenty of water. There is a small stream and pool over this way where you can fill your gourds, and here are some of my provisions which you can have for supper, so you can save the ones you have brought with you."

He approved of Lorimon's plan to start very early while the air above the sands was still cool. "Now sleep, and I will stand watch."

He did, and woke them at the first graying of the horizon. While they slept, he had filled their gourds and repacked them in the baskets. Lyn had thought to bring their fur hoods as some sort of protection against the sun, and now she found he had filled them loosely with fresh, sweet-smelling grasses which made a sort of airspace between their heads and the skins.

"I will keep watching for your return," he assured them as they gratefully thanked him for his help. "Also, I shall send word to the King that I have seen you leave."

The children's first real sight of the desert was by the feeble light of the dying moon. The sands lay dark and mysterious beneath them except where here and there a slight rippling dune gleamed faintly. It was chilly. Lyn shivered.

"I wonder if the air rising from the desert is going to be as hot as the explorers claim it is," she said to Greg. "I could use a little of that heat right now! I thought the atmosphere would keep at least some of the heat from the sand all through the night."

Lorimon heard her. "Do not worry. It will be hot, and very hot, only too soon."

As the light increased, the desert gradually turned from dark to gray and then to all shades of tan and brown. Behind them, now far in the distance, the highest of the rolling hills of the Dragon-Cousins' principality were only a dim shape. Ahead and on either side there was endless sand, barren and flat, except where capricious winds

130

had piled up curving dunes.

Lorimon told them he was flying in the direction where, according to the old tales, there was habitable land. "But whether those tales speak truly or not, no one knows. I should have asked the Master, but I did not think of it in my hurry to begin the search for my brother."

"The old tales about your forefathers coming from the North were certainly true," said Lyn, trying to sound encouraging.

"That was different. King Tolmar and his journey from the North was not just a story, but part of our history. But as to the tales about what lies beyond this desert, they may be just that . . . tales with little or no truth in them."

"As you said, the desert must end somewhere," Greg said, matter-of-factly. "At least they do in our world." He did not add aloud, though it was very much on his mind, that countless Earth travelers had perished from the heat and thirst while trying to cross those same deserts.

"Yes. But where? How far? And Dathir . . . has he found the end?"

The children could guess what he was thinking because they had whispered the same thoughts to each other. They were going to turn back in time to return safely. But what about Dathir? Had he gone on and on in despair, until it had been too late to turn back? Had he then dropped with exhaustion to the sands where he had died, or worse, lay dying?

Lorimon flew steadily, though not rapidly, all day. Each hour the glare and heat grew worse as the sun climbed higher. But that was nothing to the heat that hit them from the sand the one time Lorimon dropped down to give both himself and the children a brief rest. Dragons, being small furnaces themselves, can stand heat better than humans can, but even dragons find desert sand at noon frightfully hot. Lorimon drank a little and the children, though parched, also tried to quench their thirst with two or three mouthfuls, but they were thirsty again a few minutes later.

It was mid-afternoon, and Lyn was dizzy from the heat, when Lorimon suddenly began to fly more swiftly. "There is something far ahead," he told them. "It looks like a few trees and, if so, there must be water."

"An oasis!" Greg exclaimed, and then had to explain to Lorimon what an oasis was.

It was indeed an oasis, though a small one. There were a few trees, a patch of coarse grass and, best of all, a spring. Before they landed, Lorimon circled around it, flying very low. "See," he said, indicating some marks on the sand which looked like wide sweeps. "A dragon has been here, and not very long ago. Those marks were made by his tail. It must have been Dathir." He sounded greatly relieved. "Now that I know that we are going in the right direction, I can fly faster without having to search the sand so carefully."

"Can't we rest here for a while?" Lyn begged. "I feel baked to a crisp. I was wondering if I was going to have a sunstroke."

Lorimon agreed. "I, too, must rest and we must

drink our fill, for who knows where the next . . . what is it? . . . oasis? will be."

The spring was a small one and the pool it formed was as much sand as water, but they all plunged their heads into it and felt much better. Afterwards by patiently straining the water through Greg's shirt they were able to drink it, though it had a metallic flavor. They drank and drank and were so refreshed that they had a cheerful if meager supper in the cooler air of the evening.

"Are we going to start early?" Lyn asked Lorimon.

"As soon as the sky starts turning gray."

"If we flew at night it would be cooler," Greg objected.

"True, but then when I was tired and had to drop down, there might be no oasis and we would have to lie on the burning sands under the hot sun. I might be able to stand it, but I do not think you could. If I fly during the day, we are at least off the desert, and the air will be fairly cool when we come down in the evening, or late afternoon if I can go no farther."

"That does make sense," Lyn agreed reluctantly. She wondered if she could stand another day with that terrible heat on her head. The grass-stuffed hoods were not sufficient protection.

Greg had been thinking the same thing. He got up and picked up one of their bowl-shaped eating gourds. "Look," he put his head in the opening. "We can use these as sun helmets."

Lyn laughed; he looked so funny with the rim

balanced on his nose. "It might work! If we put our grass-stuffed hoods on first they will act as padding, and we can make a cord from the grass which will hold them on under our chins."

The next morning, before starting, they drank deeply of the filtered water. If anything, the heat was worse, though the sun helmets were a great help and Lorimon's faster wingbeats moved the air steadily around them. There was no oasis that evening and, as Lorimon had warned, they came down on the barren sand and had to use up some of their food and precious water.

It was the same the next day. Lorimon flew until evening and still there was nothing but desert stretching as far as even he could see. Once again there had been no signs of Dathir which would have given them a little hope. All were discouraged when Lorimon at last landed wearily.

"Tomorrow we must start back," he said sorrowfully. Lyn did not know what to say and so she hugged him. For some reason, that always pleased him. It did now. "You are a comfort," he said gently.

Though dead tired, Lyn slept fitfully and whenever she awoke she saw Lorimon gazing out over the desert, always in the same direction. The next morning while the children were eating a quick breakfast, she saw him again looking across the desert. His eyes were so sorrowful that she forced herself to say, because she did not want to say it at all, "Couldn't we go on at least part of the day before turning back?"

His expression brightened. "Yes, we could. If necessary I could manage to fly the last stretch to the oasis without water. We will fly until the sun reaches its full height and then, I promise, we will turn back."

So on they flew.

"Why did you give him that false hope?" Greg whispered crossly in her ear as the familiar heat grew worse.

"I had to," Lyn whispered back. "I don't know why, but I had to. He looked so sad."

"He will look even sadder when he has to turn back anyway," Greg grunted even more crossly. He was cross because he was as fond of Lorimon as Lyn was, and thought the kindest thing would be to end this fruitless search quickly.

The sun was nearly overhead when Lorimon cried out, "I see something! I think they are mountains!" He rose higher and flew faster. "Yes, they *are* mountains!"

"They may be barren and rocky like some of those we saw in the north," Greg said pessimistically.

"They are still too far away for me to see plainly," said Lorimon

"I wasn't just trying to be a wet blanket," Greg said in a low and worried voice to Lyn.

"I know what you mean," she answered. She, too, was anxious. What would they do if they did not find water?

It was not long before they also saw a faint, jagged line against the sky, a line that shimmered and wavered in the ghastly heat. To their immense relief, Lorimon soon called back over his shoulder, "They are covered with trees."

He landed, saying, "Let us take a good drink, then I shall be able to fly more swiftly, for there is still a long way to go." After nearly emptying the water gourds, they went on.

Ahead of them the outline grew larger and darker. Slowly the darkness turned into the most beautiful green Lyn thought she had ever seen, the green of living trees. Then the last of the desert passed beneath them and with its passing, fresh, cool air flowing down from the slopes enveloped them. They gulped it in and a few minutes later landed beside a crystal clear stream that gurgled along its rocky bed. They tumbled off Lorimon in their haste to bury their faces in the cool water. Afterwards, they flung themselves down in the grass, content to just lie there and be grateful for the trees and all fresh, green things.

"Let's stay here until tomorrow," said Lyn after they had been resting a short time. She stretched herself contentedly. "It's afternoon already."

"No," said Lorimon. "We came to search and search we must as long as there is light."

"But the sun is nearly down," objected Greg, who also had no desire to get up. "There will be plenty of time tomorrow."

Lorimon paid no attention to his objections; he simply adjusted the carrying pad and slid the loops of the carrying baskets around his neck.

"Oh, all right," said Greg, getting up very

slowly, "though I don't see why we can't wait until tomorrow."

Lyn was still lying on the grass and was about to add her own objections, and not too agreeably, when Lorimon said, "Get up!" so firmly that Lyn did so, more promptly than she had intended to.

They had only been moments in the air when Lorimon came down again farther up the same stream. "Look," he said, pointing at marks in the soft banks. "A dragon was here several days ago."

"Why do you think so?" Greg said, peering at the marks. "I only see hoof prints, and lots of them. This must be a drinking place for deer or some small animal like them."

"Look over here: on the very edge of the hoof prints are the marks of a dragon. They have been partly obliterated. One more evening of the deer gathering to drink and they probably would have been trampled over."

The children looked at him in chagrin, and Greg said, "Lorimon, you were right. It's a good thing we kept going."

No further signs were found, though Lorimon searched carefully until the light faded, and flew back and forth calling, "Dathir! Dathir!" Nevertheless, they were all much more cheerful as they gathered around a fire and ate the remainder of their provisions.

CHAPTER 9
The Dangerous Ruins

The pattern of the next few days was always the same. As soon as it was light, Lorimon would start sweeping low, back and forth, looking for signs and calling out his brother's name. Sometimes he hovered over a tree-covered spot which looked the same to Lyn and Greg as any other similar place. In answer to their questions, he said, "This is a place where a dragon would like to rest." He went high up the slopes, and deep into valleys, but there was no answer to his calls or any sign of Dathir. One rocky valley left Lyn terribly depressed because his calls, "Dathir! Dathir!" echoed mournfully from cliff to cliff like an ill omen.

Lorimon never left them alone. "This is a strange country and we do not know what dangers may be lurking." During the day they only saw harmless animals, deer and mountain sheep and goats. At night, though, the woods came alive with rustles and every now and then there was the death scream of some small animal. Once they heard the grunt of a bear and another night the distant howl of a wolf, but mostly just small animals. "I know their sound well," Lorimon reassured them. When he hunted, he left them in an open field or some other safe place where he could keep an eye on them and fall like a thunderbolt on any predator who came too close to them.

On one such occasion, he told them to climb part way up a rock formation. As they waited for him, they watched a pair of extremely large eagles who were circling gracefully above them. They sat so still that the eagles came lower and lower, searching for food. At last, one of them dropped on a fat rabbit in front of the rocks. Before it could rise again with its prey, however, a large serpent lashed out from behind a short, thick shrub and partially encircled the poor eagle, who screamed and vainly tried to beat itself free. Its mate flew down screaming and attacked the serpent with its beak. Greg grabbed a large stone and scrambled down while Lyn shouted for Lorimon.

The serpent had half its body coiled around the eagle when Lorimon swooped down and, taking careful aim, seared the lower half of its body with a blast of flame. With a fearful hiss the snake swiftly uncoiled and struck futilely at Lorimon, who finished it off with another hot flame. He swung his head around in a circle, keeping it close to the ground, and struck out at another snake lurking behind the same bush, which only his keen eyes had seen.

After one more rapid glance around, he turned to the eagle who was lying on the ground, gasping and feebly moving its wings. Its mate was perched on a rock calling anxiously but afraid to go any closer. Lorimon spoke gently to the injured bird and added a few soft noises. The bird lay still and looked at him, while its mate ventured closer.

"They seem to understand you!" Lyn exclaimed in astonishment. "Do you know their language?"

"No, but there are eagles, especially in the northern half of our land, and we dragons have always gotten on very well with them. They know we are friends. Why, until a few passings ago, there was an old pair who had a nest in a tree near the palace. Every day they came down for a meal the cook put out for them, and each year when their young made their first flight, the parents proudly brought them to show the King and Queen."

He spoke again to the eagles and this time they responded. "It is the she-eagle who is hurt," he said. "She undoubtedly has young at this time of year. They need her. Let us see what we can do to help. Greg, get the medicines out of the basket. You know best how to use them."

Greg's help could not be easily given. The eagles had lost their fear of Lorimon, but not of this strange, upright being. It took much coaxing from Lorimon before Greg could touch the injured bird without her struggling with fright and her mate threatening to peck him. At last both birds were quiet and following Lorimon's instructions. Greg gently moved the bird's wings until Lorimon was satisfied that they were not broken and there was no serious injury. She was, however, too badly bruised to be able to fly, and so Greg carefully rubbed the healing ointment on her wings and ribs. Lyn poured water into a small gourd for the eagle to drink and added a few drops of a remedy that Greg said was strengthening.

"What shall we do with her now?" Greg asked. "If she would let me carry her in my arms while you fly, we could get her back to her nest. It must be in a safe place."

In the end it was Lyn who held the bird. After much reassuring from Lorimon, the eagle allowed Greg to pick her up. Lyn climbed onto Lorimon and Greg carefully laid the bird in her arms, then sat behind her and steadied her. The male eagle either did not understand what Lorimon wanted or was reluctant to show them his eyrie. He trailed behind them, carrying the rabbit his mate had caught, while Lorimon circled twice looking in every direction.

"I think it is probably over there," he said, heading towards a high cliff.

He was right. A wide ledge ran curving around the cliff for a couple hundred feet. At one end it was easily wide enough for a dragon to land, and at the other and narrower end was the eyrie. Lorimon landed without the least jolt. Greg slid off and Lyn carefully handed down the mother eagle to him. He carried her along the ledge to the large nest of sticks and twigs where two partly feathered eaglets were expressing their hunger loudly. The eagle gave a faint cry at the sight of her fledglings. Greg placed her very gently beside them and made her as comfortable as he could, while the father distracted the attention of the youngsters by feeding them. When they had quieted down a bit, the father flew off and came back a good while later with another rabbit, quite a small one.

"He is going to have hard work feeding both his hungry children and their mother," commented Lyn sympathetically.

"Maybe I can help him, and I will not have to worry about you two as you are safe up here," replied Lorimon. Off he went and came back with a wild goat which he gave to the eagles. On another trip he brought up a gourdful of water for the mother who had recovered enough to give a little croak of appreciation.

During the next few days Greg tended her as he had seen the Healers tend the wounded dragons. In a couple of days she was able to move about and in another three she could fly, though stiffly, and was helping her tired mate care for the eaglets. They had completely lost their fear of the children and hopped around them unconcernedly. With Lorimon, however, it was different.

"Lorimon was right; there *is* a real understanding between him and the eagles," said Lyn to her brother one day as they watched the eagles fly up and greet the returning dragon with welcoming screams which he returned with waves of his head.

"There certainly is. I don't know how it works, but yesterday when I commented on their greeting him, he said, 'Yes, they are good friends of mine now.' And he said it as though that was perfectly normal."

During the eagle's recovery, Lorimon did not stop looking for his brother. He searched systematically, working in a circle with the eyrie as its center. Back and forth he swept over the forests and fields and into little blind valleys, always calling, "Dathir, my brother, come to me!"

On two different searches, the father eagle flew beside him, watching him closely. Finally one day, when the mother eagle was well on the way to recovery, he jerked his head in a short, sharp manner and gave several harsh calls, then flew off, looking over his shoulder.

"He wants us to follow him!" cried Greg to Lorimon.

"You are right! He realizes we are hunting for something, and my heart tells me he will give us good guidance."

The eagle led them in a direction Lorimon had not yet explored, deep into the foothills, until they came to a broad, almost circular valley. The moment Lyn saw the valley, she didn't like it. Why, she didn't know; it was much the same as the other valleys, but there was something wrong about it.

"I don't like this place," she whispered to Lorimon, leaning forward so that Greg would not hear.

"I do not either. There is something evil here. Look – the eagle thinks so, too."

The eagle had flown to the center of the valley and was circling down, giving warning cries as he did so. Below them were the ruins of what had once been a large, stone building. So ruined was it, that only a few walls were even half-standing, and the two remaining arched entrances were leaning over at a dangerous angle, as though ready to fall at any moment. The paved floor alone was fairly intact.

Huge cracks were crisscrossing its paving stones and two or three dark, gaping holes showed there must be passages under it. Lorimon circled low as he examined it.

"How strange. It looks as though it had been abandoned long ago and yet there are no vines or other growth running over it," said Greg.

"These ruins were covered with vines," said Lorimon. "See, they have only recently been torn off." He motioned to where a few vines still clung to the walls. Then he gave a sharp exclamation and dropped down more hurriedly than either Greg or Lyn liked. Under some nearby trees lay a dragon.

"Dathir!" he cried and stopped short.

It was indeed Dathir, but so changed. Instead of the trim, dashing, young dragon they had known, was a thin, dispirited dragon with lusterless eyes. Worst of all, he no longer wore the gold armband.

"Dathir, my brother! What dreadful thing has happened to you? What are you doing here, and where is your armband?" Lorimon cried out, affectionately tapping him with his head.

For a long time Dathir made no reply, then he answered in a low voice, "I am no longer worthy to wear it. You know how I disgraced the pledge I made when our father gave it to me."

"That is no reason to give it up!" Lorimon responded vigorously. "Come back with us and start afresh!"

Dathir shook his head listlessly. "The Master of this place is right. I am not worthy to wear the armband, nor can I go back. All I am fit for is to remain here and serve him until I die."

His hopeless tone stabbed Lyn to the heart and she could guess with what anguish Lorimon heard his reply.

"Who is this one you call your Master? We Green Dragons have no master except the Master of Wisdom, and he would never give you such advice. You well know that!"

"He is the Master of this place," said Dathir in the same dull, hopeless tone. He closed his eyes and laid down his head. Lorimon spoke urgently to him in a low voice. Dathir slightly lifted his head, but after one or two replies, laid it down again and made no further answer.

Lyn and Greg had drawn away in order to leave the brothers alone. Greg climbed up on a broken arch to look around. Lyn was too upset to bother with the ruins and wandered about, not noticing where she was going until she came up against a ruined wall. Without much interest she idly glanced over it and stopped, open-mouthed. Below was what had once been a courtyard. The paving stones were cracked and broken and weeds were growing through the cracks. But scattered over the stones as though flung there long ago by some careless, giant hand, were huge emeralds, rubies, diamonds, and other precious jewels. Some were as large or larger than those in the Green Dragons' Coronation collars. They were glittering in the sun like a myriad of rainbows, and looked as though they had been lying there untouched for ages.

Forgetting all caution, Lyn scrambled over the

wall and down into the courtyard as fast as she could. She could hear Greg calling from his ruined arch, "Be careful! Better not go down there until Lorimon is with us!" But she was already in the courtyard and paid no attention to him.

She picked up the first jewel she saw at her feet. It was an immense diamond. She was gazing at it in amazement when a voice close to her said, "What are you doing here?"

She spun around and saw gazing at her from a low archway the cold, slate eyes of a serpent. From the size of its head, she guessed it must be enormous. It held her with its eyes. Try as she would, she could not get free of them. She could only stand there, frozen in place.

"What are you doing here and who are you?" the voice said again. The serpent came part way into the courtyard and Lyn gulped in horror. It was indeed immense and had dull, red scales.

"Why are you taking my stone?"

"I was just looking at it," stammered Lyn, dropping the diamond hastily. "I'm sorry, I didn't know they belonged to anyone."

"They are mine." The voice was rasping and cold. "Do you want one of these stones?" The serpent had drawn closer and was looking down at her with its eyes half closed.

"Not if they are yours, of course," said Lyn, partly reassured by its use of the word 'stones'. He doesn't know their value either, she thought. She went on, "I think they are pretty, and I like pretty things." Just because he is a serpent doesn't mean that he is automatically evil, she told herself. Just think how wrongly Green Dragons were judged on Earth! But she was still uneasy. Something was wrong, very wrong.

"Well, then, since you find them pretty, you may take one."

"*Any* one?" Her desire for the jewel was silencing her deep-down fears.

"Any one you want. I give it to you freely," said the serpent, settling back and closing its eyes sleepily.

She hastily began looking over the jewels. She picked one up and laid it down again. This emerald was gorgeous, but that ruby over there was bigger; and she did love sapphires, but she quickly passed them over. None were large enough. In the end, she chose another diamond that was even larger than the first. It was so big that it filled the palm of her hand.

She heard Greg calling her. "Here I am," she called back and hurriedly climbed up out of the courtyard and over the wall. She was grateful to the serpent for being so generous, but she still did not feel quite safe.

Lorimon landed beside her. "Lyn," he began, then saw the serpent and stopped. "Who are you?" he demanded.

The serpent opened its eyes, raised its head, and stared at the dragon with such a cold, cruel look that Lyn shuddered to think she had been so close to him.

"I am the Master," he said insolently. "Have you

also come to serve me?"

"What have you done to my brother?" Lorimon demanded.

"Nothing," replied the serpent. "Or rather . . . ," he paused to coil and uncoil himself nonchalantly, "nothing that he did not let happen to him. He is now my servant."

"How did you enslave him? No Green Dragon gives up his freedom willingly!"

The serpent made a rasping, metallic noise that sounded like a horrible, mocking laugh. "He gave up his freedom willingly because he realized he was no longer worthy to wear what you call your armband and that he was fit only to be a slave. He is very useful. It is a long time since the vines were cleared off my palace, and I dislike seeing it overgrown. I also enjoy having someone who can hunt for me and spare me the trouble of finding my own food. He also brings me water and anything else I may wish. Though, judging from his thinness, I doubt if I shall have that pleasure for long. But even if only for a short time, it is . . . well . . . comfortable."

Lorimon lunged at him, breathing fire, but the serpent whisked himself away through the arch before he could land. Lorimon leaped out of the courtyard, his eyes blazing with anger. "What has he done to my brother?" he cried out in anguish. "How has he gotten such control over him?"

Lyn recalled uncomfortably how the serpent's eyes had held her. "In our world there is a way of controlling people called 'brainwashing'."

"What is that?" Lorimon asked.

Greg and Lyn tried to explain it to him as best as they could. Afterwards, Lorimon was silent a long time, thinking. "Now I begin to understand," he said at last. "When Dathir landed here, despairing and heartbroken, tired both in mind and body, this evil serpent met him with false sympathy and carefully chosen words that seemed fair, but really only increased his misery and self-contempt. Perhaps in the beginning, in pretended hospitality, he may have even given Dathir some sort of drink that dulled his mind, as our Healers sometimes do to dull the pain of a severely injured dragon. Mybrother would have suspected nothing for, as you know, we always offer guests a refreshing drink. Then by what you call 'brainwashing', this evil one gained such control of my brother's mind that he was able to make him feel he was fit for nothing except to be his slave."

"Why do you think Dathir removed his armband?" questioned Greg.

"You heard what he said about being unworthy. The serpent must have found out how much the armband means to us, and persuaded him to take it off because of his unworthiness to wear it. How does one break this evil power in your world?"

Unfortunately, neither of the children knew. Lyn thought she had read somewhere that sometimes one could be jolted out of it, or that it did eventually wear off.

"But, if so, I am certain the serpent keeps renewing it," said Greg despondently.

Lorimon nodded sadly. They went back to Dathir, but nothing any of them said could rouse him. Finally Lorimon said abruptly, "Let us go back to the eagle's eyrie. There is nothing more we can do just now."

They flew back in silence, and for a long time Lorimon just lay on the broad part of the ledge, thinking, thinking, thinking. When the children fell asleep, he was still lying there, completely still.

The next morning he said, "I have thought long and deeply, and have decided that the serpent's evil hold on my brother can only be broken either by the serpent's own death, or by Dathir's recovering his armband."

"What good would the armband do?" Greg asked. "After all, it's just a symbol, isn't it?"

"Yes, but for us it is a very powerful symbol and one with deep meaning. None of us ever forget the pledge we made when it was given to us, and we are all taught to ponder on the words, passing after passing. In this way their meaning becomes wider and deeper to us, until we at last take the Blue Road Home. I feel certain that if we could find it and persuade Dathir to repeat the oath, his heart and mind would be freed." Lorimon gazed out over the valley and repeated the oath:

My father, I promise to be brave, to be courteous, and to be faithful to the laws the Great One has laid down for the Green Dragons. I accept this gold band and will not forget that one day

150

I shall have to lay it down with all the time of my passings on it.

Lyn and Greg had several times been present at a young dragon's armbanding and had heard the words of the oath, but never spoken so solemnly or with so much meaning. He has pondered on it long and earnestly, Lyn said to herself. And she knew that if Dathir had done the same, he would never have fled.

The serpent's hold on Dathir had at first so frightened Lyn that as soon as she got back to the eyrie she wrapped the diamond in her handkerchief and hid it in a crack in the cliff. It was not until the next evening that she showed it to Greg and Lorimon.

"Where did you get it?" Greg exclaimed in astonishment, examining it closely. "I wonder if it's real?"

She told him.

He was alarmed. "I wish you hadn't taken it. I don't think anything coming from that serpent could be good."

Lorimon agreed. "That serpent is evil. Throw it away, Lyn, or let me drop it back into the courtyard the next time I fly over."

"No, indeed!" protested Lyn. "I didn't steal it! He has been wicked to Dathir, but he didn't try to hold *me*. On the contrary, he said, 'I give it to you freely'."

"Nevertheless, I don't trust him," Lorimon said fiercely. Then he added curiously, "Why do you want it so much?"

"I like it because it is pretty and I want to give it to my mother," Lyn answered evasively.

Lorimon said nothing, but looked hard at her.

"Don't look at me as though you didn't believe me!" she said angrily, and went on rapidly (because she was afraid that he might reply that he didn't), "I'm going to leave it tucked in this crack. It can't cause any trouble there. Maybe in the end I won't take it back with me," she said, trying to sound as though she didn't much care one way or the other about it. "Come on, Greg, let's see how the eaglets are coming along. I think they are going to start flying soon."

Day after day, Lorimon returned to the ruins to speak with his brother. Usually he went alone, but sometimes he took Lyn and Greg to see if they could think of something that might rouse Dathir from his lethargy. Once in a while Dathir would weep when Lorimon spoke earnestly and affectionately to him, but mostly he only sighed and repeated what he had said on that first day.

At last Lorimon said, "I will try one more time tomorrow. If I fail, we will go back and I shall seek counsel from the Master. Perhaps he can give me words or deeds by which I may hope to break these bonds of mind and heart with which the serpent holds my poor brother captive. Then I shall return and try again and again as long as one of us lives."

Greg was startled at the idea. "You mean you will remain here permanently?"

"As long as he needs me," Lorimon said simply.

"What about Alamirna?" Lyn asked anxiously.

Lorimon sighed. "I shall tell her not to wait for me but to choose someone else."

Lyn did not think Alamirna would easily accept that solution, but she saw that his mind was made up and it would be no use to argue.

That night she took the huge diamond from its crack in which she had hidden it, and made a small bag for it from her handkerchief. Greg had changed his mind about keeping it.

"I guess the serpent was in a good mood that day, and since they are just colored stones to him, he amused himself by letting you have one," he said.

While she was making the bag, he examined the diamond carefully. He held it up to the light and turned it this way and that. In the end he said, "It looks pretty badly flawed to me. See all the lines running through it? Too bad you didn't choose an emerald or a ruby. Deep green emeralds or deep red rubies – the kind called pigeon blood rubies – are rarer than diamonds and more valuable."

Lyn had already been regretting not having taken more time when choosing the jewel.

"I didn't have time," she complained. "I had to choose in a hurry. If I had another chance, I would be able to take a better one."

She had not really given any thought to having another chance, but now she did. Never, never, she told herself, would she dare go down into that courtyard again if she thought the serpent was any-where near. Yet several times they had seen him at

153

the opposite end of the long ruins, sunning himself in a warm nook. If he were there, she could safely dart down, choose another jewel, and dash out again.

Twice Lorimon had tried to catch him there unawares but was unsuccessful. The serpent heard his approach and retreated under an arch in the pavement where Lorimon could not reach him. From that safe place he spoke as long as Lorimon wanted.

"After all," he said with his horrible, harsh, rasping laugh, "I so rarely have company, that I enjoy visitors, even insulting ones like you."

All three were sad and discouraged at the failure of their hopes. Greg was especially miserable with the misery that comes from the endless repetition of, "If only I hadn't done it."

He had spent half the night trying to think up a new way of rousing Dathir.

CHAPTER 10
The Gold Armband

Dathir was lying in his usual place on this last day and, as they circled down, Lyn saw the serpent sunning himself over in that far corner.

"I am going to challenge him once more in the name of the Great One," Lorimon said thoughtfully. "Each time before, he has answered either because he had to or because some inner hatred drove him to."

He left them near Dathir. Greg at once began expounding to him all the heroic deeds of great dragons that he had ever heard of, urging Dathir to be like them.

As for Lyn, the moment she saw Lorimon speaking with the serpent, she ran over to the jewel-strewn courtyard and climbed down into it. She took the huge diamond out of her handkerchief and held it as she rapidly examined the scattered jewels. There is no harm in exchanging it for another, provided I don't take a larger one, she told herself. Which should she take, a ruby or an emerald? Next the thought came to her that it would be easier to sell several small stones. As long as the total number of jewels did not exceed in size the huge diamond the serpent had given her, it would be the same, she convinced herself, and in this way she could have both emeralds and rubies. Anyway, what right had the serpent to claim this place as his own? These jewels probably didn't belong to him or anyone else.

She held a magnificent emerald to the light. As she did so, she happened to glance at the archway that led from the courtyard to the passages below the pavement. Lying beside it was Dathir's armband. She realized at once that after obtaining it from Dathir, the serpent had dropped it there as of no further interest to him. She started towards it, then her eye was caught by the gleam of the deepest red ruby she had yet seen. She stopped to pick it up; then a gorgeous deep blue sapphire; and then another emerald . . . .

A shadow fell across the sparkling pile in her hand and the serpent's rasping voice said, "Why have you come back, and why are you taking my stones?"

He was coiled beside her, his large head a little above hers. Terrified, she looked up and again his eyes held hers locked to his.

The head swayed closer to hers. "Answer me. I gave you one . . . why have you come back to steal more?"

"I am not stealing them," she said desperately, knowing she was pleading for her life. "You were so kind and generous in giving me that one, I didn't think you would mind a bit if I exchanged it for several smaller ones. See? All of these together aren't as big as the one you gave me. I will put them all back at once if you want, and not take any."

She tried to drop the jewel-filled handkerchief but her hands were as if frozen around it. She found to her horror that she, too, was frozen in place.

The evil head swayed back and forth.

"I gave you one because it amused me to do so. I knew that if I gave it to you, you would come back for more, because there was greed for them in your eyes."

His head swung in a circle around her, keeping his eyes fixed on hers, and she found she was forced to turn also.

"What are you going to do with me?" she whispered through stiff lips.

"That dragon will soon die. Perhaps I shall make you carry my water. Or I may fatten you . . . if I am hungry."

His head circled again, drawing her with it, then he stopped and asked curiously, "What do you want the stones for?"

She had to answer. "They would bring many nice things in my world."

"What sort of things?"

"A bigger house, for instance."

"The one you have is not big enough?" he questioned.

"It is big enough for us," she answered in the same stiff whisper. Vaguely in the distance she heard Greg calling, but he couldn't help her.

"What else?"

"Beautiful clothes, cars, and things like that."

"You do not have enough of these things, whatever they are?"

"Yes," she answered miserably, "but others have more."

"Ah!" The serpent's head circled her once more and then he drew back as though to strike her. Abruptly, he turned away from her with a scream of pain. Lorimon's fiery breath had hit him. He lunged at the hovering dragon who dropped down and lunged back.

With the breaking of his gaze Lyn knew she was free. The handkerchief full of jewels dropped from her hands.

"Run, Lyn, run!" cried Lorimon.

Shaking from the suddenness of her release, she took one step towards the wall, then remembered the armband. She glanced over her shoulder; the serpent's tail was between her and the archway. She couldn't reach the armband without jumping over it and he might lash out at her. There flashed across her mind Lorimon's anguished face as he pleaded with Dathir, and Dathir's hopeless eyes. She hesitated a split second more, then jumped across the thrashing tail and grabbed the armband. As she darted back she narrowly missed being crushed against the wall as the serpent drew back before lashing out again at Lorimon.

She dashed across the courtyard and scrambled as fast as she could up the wall. Greg raced up to her as she climbed over it.

"Here is the armband!" she cried, shoving it into his hands. "Get it to Dathir quickly and make him repeat the pledge! Run! Run!" she shouted after him. "If the serpent gets away from Lorimon he may try to kill Dathir in revenge!"

Greg needed no urging. He tore over to Dathir.

"Look!" he said commandingly. "Here is your armband! You must put it on again at once!"

Dathir's head came up and a light began to come back into his eyes as he stared at it.

"Put your arm out as you did for your father!"

Dathir did so in a dazed manner.

In the same commanding tone, Greg went on, "Recite the pledge after me!" He slipped the armband on and began, "My father, I promise to be brave, to be courteous . . ."

"My father, I promise . . ." repeated Dathir, hesitatingly at first, and then more and more firmly with the light growing in his eyes as he said it. At the end he looked bewildered for a moment, then said in a low voice, "I am free."

Lyn raced up, shouting, "Quick! Lorimon is fighting for his life!"

Dathir's eyes snapped awake. "Lorimon fighting for his life!" and he shot up into the air. Before he reached the wall, Lorimon had leapt out of the courtyard and in two wingbeats was on the ground beside them.

"Lorimon, I am free, free!" cried Dathir. He was weeping.

Lorimon stared at him and at the gold armband. "Just when I had given up all hope!" he said, and there was a choke in his voice. "But no time for more now. The serpent is infuriated and may be upon us at any moment."

His warning did not come a moment too soon.

The children flung themselves on his back and as he cleared the ground the serpent shot out of a nearby concealed opening with a furious hiss. He managed to throw himself over the end of Lorimon's tail but could not coil himself around it sufficiently to drag Lorimon down again. Lorimon shook himself free, and with Dathir beside him, rose up over the ruins, leaving the scorched serpent writhing and hissing in futile anger.

Back at the eyrie the twins left the dragons on the broad ledge and tactfully retreated around the curve to the eagles' nest. They could hear the brothers speaking. In between there were extra-long dragon silences. At length Lorimon called them back. Dathir looked at them anxiously as though he wondered how they would greet him, and so before he could say a word Lyn hugged him, which she had never done before, and Greg thumped him on the back, saying, "I'm sorry, Dathir. It was my fault."

Dathir placed his head gently against each of their cheeks and said, "No, it was my fault. Moreover, how can I ever thank both of you? Next to Lorimon, my beloved brother, you have been the ones who released me from the bonds that bound me to that evil serpent. Bonds which were of my own making," he added sorrowfully.

"I think it was your love for Lorimon that really freed you in the end," said Greg, sitting down beside him. "The instant Lyn cried out that he was fighting for his life, you snapped out of your . . . your . . . daze."

"It was both. When you gave me the armband and started to recite the words of the pledge, a darkness began to lift from my heart and mind. Then at Lyn's cry the last of the mist fled and I was free."

He bent his head and tears rolled down his cheeks. "I dishonored my pledge, more by my lack of trust than by what I did. In my pride and bitterness, I let myself forget that to those who honor the Great One, there is always a way back from shame and disgrace."

"You *have* come back, and that is what matters," said Lorimon. "Now tell us what happened, Lyn. How did you find the armband? After I had spoken uselessly to the serpent, I went to Dathir and was speaking equally uselessly to him when Greg raced over shouting that you were in the serpent's clutches."

"I had given up on trying to convince Dathir," added Greg, "and when Lorimon left the serpent I went over to the courtyard to see what you were doing. When I saw the serpent circling you, with you following his every movement, I ran yelling for Lorimon! If only I could sprint like that at school, I would win every race," he finished, laughing.

Lyn did not want to tell her ignominious part and nearly said, which was true as far as it went, that she had wanted to take another look at the jewels. Then she told herself firmly, Dathir and Greg have both said they're sorry, and I'm going to do the same. So she told her whole part, ending with a gulp, "I should have taken the armband as soon as I saw it, but I wanted the jewels; and then it was almost too late."

"But not too late," Lorimon said gently.

"I nearly didn't go back for it," Lyn confessed.

"Yet you *did* have the courage to go back in the face of great danger, and did so for love of Dathir and myself. Let us remember that and forget the rest."

"Right now," he went on, spreading his wings, "Dathir needs a good meal and so do we. I am going hunting."

It was an unusually long time before he returned with a deer.

"I no longer dare to hunt anywhere except in the open," he told them. "That evil serpent is now infuriated. As you know, there are many snakes lurking in the woods and thickets, and everywhere there is long grass. I do not know if he has any sway over them, but I dare not take any chances."

That first meal back together was a very happy one, even though no one said much. Greg, who was a better cook than his sister, made the best soup he could manage. The venison was well-rubbed with herbs before being roasted, and Lyn the previous day had picked quantities of late summer berries and plums. Everyone agreed it was one of the best dinners they had ever had, though Greg suspected they would have said the same even if he had burned everything to a crisp. They were all so happy!

The next few days dragged by slowly for Greg and Lyn. Except for a short flight now and then,

Lorimon would not permit them to leave the safety of the eyrie. Most of the time they were alone, for Lorimon was out on long hunts and Dathir was spending more and more time flying as he worked to regain his strength so that he could cross the desert.

At first he merely swept back and forth, mounting and falling in broad spirals. In a short time, however, he was once again doing all the fancy wing exercises. Lyn saw right away, however, that he was doing them very differently now, as she watched him from her perch in the eyrie. There were no extra acrobatics, only the normal warrior exercises, repeated over and over again, carefully and thoroughly.

Greg noticed the change also. "I used to admire his elaborate stunts so much, especially because none of the other warriors did them. Now, I realize that these plain everyday exercises are the more important. The others are, well, just that – stunts."

"Poor Dathir. What a hard lesson he has had, but he certainly has learned it!"

Greg nodded, not taking his eyes off Dathir. "I only hope I have learned mine."

"And I, mine." They were silent for a moment, then she grinned at Greg. "Remember the first days we were here, how we decided that on this visit we were just going to have a good time?" They both laughed, and jumped up to wave a greeting to Lorimon who was returning to the eyrie with one of his eagle friends riding on his back.

Fortunately their boredom didn't last very long. Dathir was soon back to full strength and all were anxious to leave. The dragons said the return trip would be easier and shorter. Since there were two of them, they would be able to take twice as much water and provisions and, as on the northern trip, they would take turns carrying Lyn and Greg. Besides, they would go faster as no time would be lost searching.

The day before they planned to leave, at the twins' request, they took a long flight deep into the land. Now that their anxiety and grief were gone, they were able to enjoy the thick woods and flowering fields.

"If this place had more streams and rivers and ponds, it would be very much like your land, wouldn't it?" Lyn said to Dathir, upon whom they were riding.

"No, indeed!" he said vigorously and emphatically. "Absolutely not! I can assure you, once I am back there, I am never going to leave again!" But he chuckled at their laughter.

"What about you, Lorimon?" Greg called over to him.

"I agree with my brother completely. I am glad we went north and . . . yes, I am glad we went south. But our land is where I belong."

On their way back to the eyrie they flew close to the serpent's ruined palace. Dathir veered over to it, looked about, and said to Lorimon, "It would ease my heart greatly if we could destroy this evil monster so that he could do no more harm – and I think we can. The section where he usually dwells is nearly in ruins also. If we knocked over one or two of its leaning walls, they might crash down upon him. Even if they did not strike him, he might try to flee the building. If so, that entrance over there is the one from which he would probably try to escape as it is closest to the forest. That leaning arch is right above it, and if we are swift and dexterous, we can topple it down upon him as he flees."

Lorimon, somewhat reluctantly, agreed. Lyn and Greg were stationed safely on high parts of the ruin and told to keep watch in case the serpent tried to escape in another direction.

First the dragons took up heavy pieces of the ruins and dropped them with thunderous crashes on the part of the pavement beneath which Dathir thought the scorched serpent might be lying. Nothing happened.

"Let us try that wall," said Lorimon, who was warming up to the work. He motioned towards a towering remnant. Exerting all their strength, they managed to loosen it and it crashed down through the pavement beneath. A muffled shriek came through the shattered stones. The dragons leapt towards the opening crying out, "The Great One and the King!" and threw themselves against the leaning arch, toppling it over just as the head of the serpent slithered into view. His harsh shriek was broken off and there was silence.

The dragons hovered for a few minutes, looking at him; then Lorimon called over, "He is dead!"

When the children clambered down from their

perches, Lyn found she was beside the courtyard of jewels. As she stood looking at the gems that seemed a fire of colors in the brilliant sunshine, Lorimon dropped down beside her.

"I can see why you want one for your mother," he said. "Some of them are as beautiful as those in our Coronation collars. Take some if you want! They belong to nobody, now."

Lyn took a step forward and stopped. Lorimon, she knew, saw only their beauty; her world would count their value. What would it be like to own the most valuable jewels in her world; to always have to worry about guarding them? Would her mother still sing around the house and in her beloved garden? Would she still have time to keep an eye on eighty-six-year-old Mrs. Brendan who lived alone? What would it do to all of them?

Resolutely, she turned away. Let them remain there gleaming in the sun as they had for untold passings. Beautiful – that was the way she would remember them. She walked away rapidly without looking back, afraid that if she did she might regret her decision.

Later, when she told Greg, he agreed completely. "Why, we might have become so grand, that we would have turned up our noses at people like the James'. Besides, think of all the professional thieves who would have been on our trail!"

The eagles had been watching their departure preparations intently, and upon the dragons bidding them farewell they uttered sharp, shrill cries of protest.

166

"They are trying to tell us something, but what, I do not understand," said Lorimon.

The father eagle picked up a gourd by its loop and, placing it beside one of the fledglings, shoved the youngster towards it.

"Do you think the eagles want to go with us?" asked Lyn. She took another gourd and placed an eaglet in it.

"Why, you are right!" exclaimed Lorimon, as the parents made delighted noises. When the eaglet tried to get out, the mother shoved it back in.

Dathir and Lorimon were dubious. "We would gladly take them, but it will be a hard trip for the young ones. The parents will have no trouble," said Lorimon.

"Yes, how will they stand the heat?" added Dathir. But the eagles raised such a clamor when Lorimon tried to refuse, that he finally decided to take them.

This caused a brief delay. Dathir flew off and found two more large gourds. Greg had to cut off the tops, clean them out, pad them with leaves and then fasten the tops back on with a net of vines in such a way that the birds had protection from the sun, yet plenty of air. The eaglets, protesting loudly, were placed in them and each of the dragons carried one around his neck.

Lyn and Greg dreaded the flight back over the desert, but with freshly padded gourd sun-helmets and no need to ration every drop of water, the flight to the oasis was no more than very uncomfortable.

"Tomorrow night we will be among the Dragon-

Cousins and there will be real beds," said Lyn, trying to squirm the sand into comfortable holes for her body for the night under the oasis' trees.

"Nice hot bread and fresh fruit for me," murmured Greg, contentedly, already half-asleep.

They were awakened early by shrill cries from the eagles.

"Those sound like warning cries," Greg said, jumping to his feet.

"They are," said Dathir. "Something is wrong. We, too, feel it, but we do not know what it is."

"In our world birds often cry like that before some natural disaster like an earthquake or tidal wave," commented Lyn.

"If there is going to be an earthquake, the safest place for us is in the air. Come on," said Lorimon.

While the eagles hovered overhead, still uttering their anxious cries, the children hurriedly fed the eaglets, then took a quick drink themselves and stuffed some breakfast in their pockets.

"The sooner we are across this desert, the happier I shall be," said Lyn as she settled herself on Lorimon.

"I am anxious to be across, also. Tell me if I fly too fast for your safety," he replied.

The sky was overcast and the air oppressive, but the morning wore on and nothing happened. Towards midday, Dathir, who had been flying high above them, dropped down in a magnificent warrior wing-drop, saying exultantly, "I can see faintly our Dragon-Cousins' hills!"

The general rejoicing was interrupted by fresh

cries from the eagles.

"What is that?" Dathir asked, looking in surprise at a low, whirling cloud coming up behind them. At first it was light in color, but it was rapidly growing darker and taller.

"It looks as though a wind was rising and picking up bits of sand as it passes over the desert," said Lorimon, wheeling around to watch.

"It's a sandstorm! I've never seen one, but I've heard about them," said Lyn. "They can be very terrible. Travelers get lost in them. If they are on camels," and she had to quickly explain what a camel was, "the riders make the camels crouch down and then they take shelter behind them. If not, they might be buried in the sand."

The dragons were not troubled. "We shall fly above it," said Dathir, and on they went.

Looking back, Lyn was frightened at the speed with which the storm was growing and catching up with them. The cloud that had been thin and wavering had gathered up so much sand that it was dark and lowering and very dangerous-looking. In a few minutes the front edge was swirling about them. The dragons, who were already flying high, rose higher. Lorimon, burdened by the children and afraid of rising too steeply, was engulfed by the driving sands. Fortunately, Lyn and Greg had already covered their faces, Lyn with her handkerchief and Greg with his shirt. Now they clung desperately to the pad as the fury of the storm increased and Lorimon was buffeted to and fro by the wind.

From somewhere above them, Dathir's voice came faintly. "It is too high for you, Lorimon. I have reached where the sands are thinner, but you could not."

Lyn realized he was referring to their weight. She knew that Lorimon would as little think of deserting them to save his own life, as he had when faced by the northern dragons, so she was not surprised when, after battling the winds for what seemed like hours, he called out to Dathir, "I am going to drop down and we shall attempt to live through this storm by imitating the Earth people and their camels. Hold on tightly, Lyn and Greg, I am going down through the worst of the storm." He did so, circling swiftly, and for a few moments the force of the wind nearly sucked the children off, although they were lying flat and clung with all their strength. Then they were down.

"Get under my wings," ordered Lorimon.

They felt their way, eyes tightly closed, off of Lorimon's back, and then crept under his wings, one on each side. They only realized that Dathir had come down with them when his voice said, "Here, keep these little ones with you and free them from the sand."

He shoved a gourd with an eaglet in it under each of Lorimon's wings. The poor birds were nearly buried in sand and were crying pathetically for their parents.

"Where are the eagles?" Lyn asked as Dathir's head pushing an eaglet's gourd came under the wing where she was huddled.

"Undoubtedly safe above the storm. Eagles can fly much higher than we can."

Getting her eaglet free of the sand and then trying to comfort it helped Lyn forget her own fear, but she felt nearly suffocated by the time Lorimon called out that the storm was over. He began to shake himself free of the sand piled about him. She crept out. The storm was moving away and dying out as it did so.

"That was awful! We must have been caught in the worst of it," said Greg, shaking himself vigorously. "Ugh!"

"How far are we from land?" Lyn asked, feeling as though they had indeed been at sea. She hoped it was not far; she felt sick and dizzy.

The dragons looked at each other.

"We do not know," Lorimon replied. "We have been so blown about, we are no longer certain of our direction. Dathir has already flown up, but can see nothing except sand."

"Can't you tell by the sun?" Greg asked in alarm. Although the sky was overcast, he knew the dragons would have no difficulty knowing where it was. Dragons have a marvelous sense of direction.

"Yes. But what we do not know is how far it is now across the desert, and it is urgent we go by the shortest way," Lorimon said simply. He did not have to say more. The children understood. Either they went by the shortest way, or they would never get there.

Lyn was afraid her voice would tremble so she kept quiet. Greg tried to be matter-of-fact but his voice was not quite steady as he said, "Well, then, I suppose the only thing to do is to take a drink and start off in whatever direction you think is best."

"There is no more water," Dathir replied quietly. "The wind so tore at the gourds, that they were wrenched from my neck. My eaglet was saved only because I held its gourd fast against my chest."

All were silent. "We must start now," said Lorimon gently, "and do the best we can . . . and may the Great One be with us."

In silence, the children remounted and the dragons flew towards the point they had decided upon. On and on they went. The heat grew worse. Every now and then Lyn gazed ahead, desperately at first and then hopelessly. Nothing but sand, endless burning sand. Lorimon flew lower and lower and finally landed.

"I must rest," he said.

"I will carry Lyn and Greg for a while," Dathir was saying, when shrill cries sounded above them. The eagles had found them and were flying low, giving urgent calls. Having gotten their attention, the male swung around and started over the desert. He did this twice. Hope returned: none doubted that he was showing them the best way.

Greg and Lyn changed to Dathir's back. Still nothing but sand; sand and a growing grayness which was getting darker and darker, Lyn thought, though it was still daylight. The darkness was in her head, and she felt herself letting go. What a terrible fall it will be, she thought vaguely, and so was surprised when she landed with only a small thump. Dathir had felt her slipping and had landed as she slid off. Greg was pretty much in the same condition. In a few moments they both declared they already felt better. Lyn wondered if her face was as white as Greg's.

"Dathir," Lorimon ordered firmly, "you are a swifter flier than I am. You take the eaglets and go ahead with the eagle and bring us back water. We will follow slowly."

The brothers looked at each other.

"Very well," said Dathir. He slipped out of the carrying pad and flew off. Very quickly he and his eagle guide were lost to Lyn's fuzzy sight. Above them the mother eagle was circling slowly.

"She will be a marker for Dathir when he returns," said Lorimon. "They are faithful friends." He put the carrying pad on and said, "Let us go as far as we can."

As far as we can . . . so Lorimon cannot go much farther either, Lyn thought wearily. It was only long afterwards that she realized Lorimon could have flown over the desert, but he knew that neither she nor Greg would be able to hold on. So he chose to go only as far as they could. Which was not far.

"Lorimon, I can't hang on," she whispered through lips so parched that she wondered if he heard. Either he did or he was keeping such a close watch on them that he knew their strength was gone. Down he came.

"Get under my wings," he said. They did, and he kept them slightly opened so they were like a tent with air passing through.

It is too late for Dathir to reach us; Tom will think we are drowned, were Lyn's last thoughts.

CHAPTER 11
If Only I Could See It!

"We *are* drowning," she gasped, struggling as though she were, and opened her eyes to find Dathir pouring water on her while Lorimon did the same to Greg. Dathir's sides were heaving from the speed of his flight.

"It is not far; the dust from the storm hid the trees ahead," he said when his panting had subsided.

Partly revived and tremendously cheered, the children climbed back onto Lorimon. The distance was indeed not far, but Lyn's head was aching and felt twice its normal size when at last she felt, rather than saw, the sun being cut off as they landed under some stunted but shade-giving trees by a small stream. In a moment, she and Greg were plunging their heads in the water, and the dragons were drinking deeply and splashing the water over themselves.

A voice broke through their splashings. "Well! I am glad to see you have returned safely!"

It was Wollimar, the Dragon-Cousin whom they had met before crossing the desert.

"I saw one dragon come here in a great hurry and then fly back over the desert with water, so I guessed there was trouble and that he was a rescue party. I headed towards this place, figuring you would land here and that you might like a nice, cool drink. Now all of you have a good rest while I am getting it ready."

The drink was most refreshing, though Lyn had no idea what it was made of. They all had to make do with his bowl and the one gourd that had survived the sandstorm because it had happened to be fastened extra firmly to the carrying pad. No one minded, and Lyn cheerfully did the in-between washings in the stream.

Although by this time the children were pretty well recovered, they nevertheless wanted to remain where they were for the night, but the dragons would not agree.

"It is not far from the Dragon-Cousins' land and we shall spend the night there," Lorimon said decidedly. When he used that tone of voice, they knew that he meant it.

The Dragon-Cousins welcomed them with their usual, friendly hospitality. Greg was given the hot buns he had been looking forward to and fell asleep with one only half-eaten. Lyn, without waiting for supper, laid down on the comfortable bed provided for her and did not wake up until late the next morning.

Greg was already up and waiting for breakfast, and Lorimon was chatting with a Dragon-Cousin, when Lyn joined them. Dathir was nowhere in sight.

"He left early because he wanted to speak to the King and the Master as soon as possible."

"He wanted to say he was sorry as soon as he could, didn't he?" Lyn said to Lorimon. "Brave

Dathir!"

"You are right. He is braver than he ever was and I am proud to be his brother," said Lorimon with a 'this is the end of the matter' look, so Lyn tactfully changed the subject.

The eaglets who, the night before, had appeared rather battered by their experience had also been well taken care of and were their lively selves again. Above them on a low housetop their parents were sitting with their eyes half-closed, "Looking positively overstuffed," Lyn said to Greg with a giggle.

Lorimon took them back to the palace at such a leisurely pace that it was late afternoon when they arrived. The royal family and Alan were waiting for them and warm greetings were exchanged.

The motherly Queen wept with delight at seeing them again, "which I thought I never would," she admitted.

The taciturn King said little, but his long, deep look at Lorimon and his, "It is good to have you back, my second son," with the slightest of catches in his voice, was just as expressive as the Queen's greeting.

Lorimon at once introduced the eagles who appeared to be a little overawed. The King and Queen bowed to them and welcomed them kindly, and once again Lyn witnessed the immediate understanding that existed between the dragons and eagles.

"You are most welcome," said the King, "and we shall consider it an honor if you settle within our realm."

"Do you think they would like the old nest in that tall tree over there? I still miss the eagles who used to live there," said the Queen.

"Do show them the nest, Lorimon, and then tell us how you fared," said the King. "Dathir has already told us his part. Now we are anxious to hear yours."

Lorimon led the eagles to the nest which was in full view of the palace terrace. No sooner did the eagles see it than they uttered pleased cries, and Lorimon left them busy cleaning out the accumulated debris and reinforcing the weakened places.

Back on the lawn, Lorimon briefly told the King what had happened. He praised the children highly and said nothing about Lyn's attempted theft and little about his own part. At the conclusion he looked straight at the King and said, "My uncle, Dathir has suffered much and learned much. You need no longer fear for him."

The King nodded slowly. "Yes, Dathir who is also beloved to me, has learned to live with failure and disgrace, and to look with hope beyond them. Now there is good reason to think that he may one day become a great warrior."

Lyn went over to the King and said earnestly, "Please, Your Majesty, won't you pardon him and let him be a warrior again right away? He is sorry for the past, and I know that although now he would willingly accept every penalty, he will always long to be a warrior."

"I have already remitted his penalty, for the terrible suffering he brought on himself has been a greater punishment than any I could have imposed. He knows he may return to his post in the north as soon as he wishes. I again urged him, to first spend some time on the Mount with the Master, for the bitterness of his actions is still with him, but this time he needed no urging. He is there now."

By this time the eagles had the nest ready for their young who were being patiently watched over by an elderly dragoness. But how to get them up there? No full-grown dragon could go near the nest without badly damaging the tree's branches. Finally Greg climbed up with a rope made of vines and hauled the eaglets up one by one. He gently tumbled them out of their gourds onto the nest and climbed down again, followed by the grateful cries of the contented parents.

Lorimon went off to see Alamirna and to bring her back to the family dinner. While he was gone, Lyn and Greg told the King all Lorimon had done to save his brother and them. Lyn even confessed the foolishness her desire for the jewels had led her into.

The King asked a few questions, then said, "Lorimon is right. You are both very brave and as in the time of King Damor you have been great friends to us. As to Lorimon," he paused and gave a slight chuckle, "do not tell him I said so, but he is one of the finest of our young dragons."

It was a delightful and joyous evening. Everyone was happy and there was so much to be said that it was late before anyone thought of going to bed.

"What a pleasant end to our journeys," said Greg, and then exchanged startled looks with Lyn.

The word "end" hung ominously in the air. Was this the end of their stay with the dragons?

Alan startled them even more. "Strange, when you said 'end', it was almost as though something was really ending . . . closing."

"Like the closing of a door?" Lyn said in a low voice.

Alan looked startled, too, then said sadly, "Yes, that is what it was like . . . the closing of a door." They were all silent.

The next day the feeling was stronger.

"It's no use trying to ignore it," Lyn said sorrowfully. "It won't go away and it's better for us to go now when we know we should, rather than be forced out in some way or other, as we undoubtedly would be sooner or later."

"Sooner, probably," said Greg gloomily.

"You're right," said Alan with a sigh. "For myself, I'd like to spend one more day with the Master."

"I'd like to have one more day flying all over the realm," said Greg.

"So would I," agreed Lyn. "It is also Lorimon's last day of leave. The King gave him extra time but he refused, saying he had been away from his post too long as it was. But I am going to ask the King if he can stay with us until we actually go."

So they had a final, glorious day that was all too short. The next morning they said their grateful goodbyes to the King and Queen and Prince before going to see the Master.

In a last private talk with him, Lyn told him of

her desire for the jewels because of their value in her world.

"I am truly glad I did not take them, but I know that at times I will regret it."

"You will," said the Master, "in your desires, but never in the depths of your heart. And, Child from Earth, because you did not take them when you freely could have, the things in your world will have less hold on you than on most."

Dathir was lying quietly on one side of the plateau, looking intently at the Blue Road, and he did not see them. Greg did not want to disturb him, but Lyn said she simply could not go without saying goodbye to such a dear friend. When she spoke his name he turned, and from the peace she saw in his eyes, she knew the healing of mind and heart that he so badly needed had begun.

"So you must return to your own world," he said gently. "Never will my heart forget what I owe you. You will always be one of my most cherished memories. Try not to remember me too hardly."

"You will always be to us a most dear friend," said Lyn. She hugged him hard, and so did Greg.

After a final farewell to the Master, Lorimon, at Alan's request, took them to the Blue Road. As soon as they landed on the beach, Alan, unaided, slid off Lorimon's back and again unhesitatingly went straight to the Blue Road.

"How do you know where it is?" Greg could not help exclaiming.

"Can't you *feel* it?" Alan asked in surprise. "It is so much *right here*! How beautiful it must be! If only

I could see it!" he cried in a voice full of longing, holding out his arms toward it. Tears were running down his cheeks. "If only I could see it!"

Alan, who never complained, who never felt sorry for himself; Lyn's heart ached for him and she could not speak. Nor could Greg. It was Lorimon who bent down to Alan and said gently, "Do not grieve. You will see it one day."

They all stood in the ripples for a long time, Alan with the same listening attitude he had had when he first came to Smugglers' Cove. At length he turned away with a sigh. "Let's go."

In a clearing not far from the Door, they said goodbye to Lorimon with many loving hugs from Lyn and gentle head taps from Lorimon. "How I shall miss you, dear friends!" he said. "We have been through so much together."

Lyn and Greg each took one of Alan's hands and they walked slowly towards the Door. None of them felt like talking.

Alan was the first to speak.

"This is no way to leave such a wonderful land as this," he said in almost his old, cheerful manner. His words broke the sorrowful spell and they chatted gaily until they reached the middle of the glade with the Door. There, in mutual, unspoken consent, they stopped. Alan turned his face up to the unclouded sky, drinking in the air while Lyn and Greg looked for a long, last moment at the great trees, the astonishingly green grass, and the bright flowers.

The Door opened easily at Greg's push and

suddenly Lyn knew she was glad to be returning to her own world.

"After all," said Alan, echoing her thoughts, "this is *our* world and this is where we belong. The other was only lent to us."

Greg brought the picnic basket out of the cave onto the beach, saying as he did so, "I'm glad it's been a long time since breakfast. It would be hard to explain to your mother, Alan, why we brought back a nearly full basket!"

"She'd be certain we were all dangerously ill," Alan said, laughing. "Where are the chicken sandwiches? She always puts some in for me."

Demolishing the contents of the basket in no way impeded their non-stop conversation about their adventures. Alan said he had collected quantities of marvelous dragon tales which he would tell them later.

"Will you also tell us some time what you learned from the Master?" Lyn asked. "You were so much with him."

"I will try," Alan promised, "but I'm not certain that I can. It is so much *inside* me."

He paused a little later with a half-eaten jam tart in his hand. "I hope Tom comes back soon. You say the time here was exactly the same when we came back as when we left, but as far as I'm concerned, it's been weeks and I'm anxious to see my family."

Presently, Tom's boat turned into the Cove and he was surprised to see all of them jump up and wave vigorously.

"What a grand welcome!" he called to them as

he waded ashore after dropping a small anchor. "You make me feel as though I've been away for a month! Hope the basket's not quite empty." He stopped short and stared at Alan. "What on earth has happened to you, Alan? You couldn't possibly have gotten so brown in an hour!"

Every now and then on the way back, he would turn around and stare at his brother and repeat, "It just isn't possible!" Once he caught hold of his brother's hand and examined it carefully. "You didn't rub anything on for the fun of fooling us, did you?" to the great amusement of the children who had difficulty not being convulsed with laughter.

As he tied up at the wharf he said, "Anytime you want to go back to the Cove, just tell me and I'll whisk you over."

The next day the twins happened to meet Mrs. James who could not thank them enough for having taken Alan with them. "I don't know when I've seen him look so well or so happy. He's just bubbling over! Please take him again with you sometime and I'll pack another basket."

At the first opportunity, Greg and Lyn told old Captain Manley, who knew about the dragons because his two grandchildren had told him of their own adventure going through the Door.

"Wait until Laura and David hear about this! They'll be here tomorrow for a week's visit. Come back over and tell them."

So they did. What a time they had! They talked so long that the twins had to run home to be in time for supper. As they stopped to open the Captain's gate, Greg called back, "Let's go over to the Cove tomorrow."

"All right," Laura shouted.

That night, however, one of the worst storms within the village inhabitants' memory howled across the Atlantic and beat against the coast for two days. The third morning broke clear and bright, though the sea was still heaving and tossing as the four of them went along the cliffs to Smugglers' Cove. There was no possibility of their walking around the rocks, and so they began to climb down. Suddenly they stopped, staring in dismay at the desolation below them. Part of the cliff had crumbled under the force of the storm, and where the cave had been was now a mass of tumbled rocks over which turbulent waves were breaking. They stood for a long time, silently looking. The girls could not help crying and the boys felt like it. They unhappily made their way back to the village.

"Alan will be so disappointed when he hears of this," Lyn said. "Like us, he was hoping to find the Door again."

At the edge of the village they passed by the home of the twins' uncle doctor. Their aunt was cleaning up the lawn.

"Did you hear?" she said after they had exchanged greetings. "Alan James has had another one of his heart attacks. Not a serious one, I believe, but your uncle was called over as usual."

"Let's go and find out how he is," said Lyn.

At the James' house they met their uncle coming out of the door.

"How is . . . ?" began Lyn and stopped.

Her uncle's face told them before he said gently, "He's gone. His first attack was not severe, but he had another while I was there, and he slipped away peacefully. He said he was going Home and sent everyone his love." Their uncle paused a moment. "It was strange. Just before the end, his face lit up and he looked as though for the *first* time he was actually *seeing* something. Then he said, 'The Blue Road! . . . How beautiful it is!"

THE END